The **STORY PIRATES** *present*

QUEST FOR THE CRYSTAL CROWN

The **STORY PIRATES** *present*

Stuck in the Stone Age

Digging Up Danger

The **STORY PIRATES** *present*

QUEST FOR THE CRYSTAL CROWN

Written by Annabeth Bondor-Stone
and Connor White
Illustrated by Joe Todd-Stanton

Random House New York

Visit us on the Web! rhcbooks.com

Educators and librarians, for a variety of teaching tools, visit us at RHTeachersLibrarians.com

Library of Congress Cataloging-in-Publication Data
Names: Bondor-Stone, Annabeth, author. | White, Connor, author. | Todd-Stanton, Joe, illustrator.
Title: The story pirates present: quest for the Crystal Crown / written by Annabeth Bondor-Stone and Connor White; illustrated by Joe Todd-Stanton.
Other titles: Quest for the Crystal Crown.
Description: New York: Random House, [2020] | Includes a nonfiction guide to writing fantasy.
Summary: "Laura, a magic wielder who lives in a forgotten city, ventures outside the city walls to find a magical crystal crown that's gone missing" —Provided by publisher.
Identifiers: LCCN 2019005379 (print) | LCCN 2019007864 (ebook) | ISBN 978-0-593-12063-7 (trade hardcover) | ISBN 978-0-593-12064-4 (ebook)
Subjects: | CYAC: Quests (Expeditions)—Fiction. | Magic—Fiction. | Fantasy—Fiction. Classification: LCC PZ7.1.B665 (ebook) | LCC PZ7.1.B665 Sto 2020 (print) | DDC [Fic]—dc23

Printed in the United States of America
10 9 8 7 6 5 4 3 2 1
First Edition

DEAD END
Hobbly Knobbly's Place
HILLVIEW
Wildflowers
Easy Street
Hot Breath's Bridge
MARBLE CITY
PUTRID FOREST
BOG BELLY
Goblin Cave

The **STORY PIRATES** *present*

QUEST FOR THE CRYSTAL CROWN

A BRIEF MESSAGE FROM

ANGIE ORTIZ

Kid Writer

My name is Angie. I'm eleven years old, and I'm from New York. Some of my favorite activities to do are crafts, painting, reading, writing, and cooking.

My parents moved to the United States from Guatemala twenty years ago. They have always instilled in my three sisters and me the value of a positive attitude and hard work. They encouraged me and made me feel that I can accomplish anything I put my mind to.

I was first introduced to Story Pirates when my writing

teacher, Mrs. Zweig, called me over to her desk. She told me that there was a contest on a website named Story Pirates and that I should enter it. I told her that I would. I thought nothing of it, other than just a regular "Enter to win an amazing prize" contest that I wouldn't win and then I'd just forget about it. Except that it turned out to be almost the complete opposite of what I originally thought. When I had the whole picture of what I needed to do, and how to do it, I knew that I had to work my hardest on it for the slightest chance of winning out of students from all over the country. It took me a couple of days, but when I was finished, I checked it over twice and submitted it. About four weeks later, my dad got a message saying that I was one of the three people to have a chance to win.

In the end, I would find out that I had won the contest, and I was ecstatic! My idea was going to be turned into a real book! I learned that you don't need to be an adult to write a book, and when you put in effort, like my parents taught me, something great might happen—and it did! I feel grateful to Story Pirates for this recognition and for this amazing experience.

Even though I don't plan on becoming a writer when I grow up, my career will include writing. This experience has affected me in a positive way, and I'll never forget it. Remember to dream big—you never know what might happen!

A BRIEF MESSAGE FROM

ROLO VINCENT

Captain of the Story Pirates

Hello, readers! Rolo Vincent here. Welcome to the latest Story Pirates book! We took Angie's idea for a story and turned it into a WHOLE FANTASY NOVEL!

Are you ready for a thrilling story full of heroes, villains, magic, and monsters? Then congratulations, because a story like that starts in only two pages! Wow, you really came to the right place, didn't you?

Before you go rushing off, though, I wanted to let you

know about a HUGE SECRET: There's more to this book than just an awesome story.

In the back of the book, be on the lookout for the FANTASY CREATION ZONE. It's full of ideas for how to create your *own* brand-new fantasy world and then write a story about a hero going on an exciting adventure there! In fact, while you read *Quest for the Crystal Crown,* Angie and I will be popping up on the page every now and then to tell you about something cool you might want to check out back in the FCZ—like in the chapter where there's a big monster fight, we'll let you know where to go if you want to find out how to write a monster fight of your own!

Want to see what I'm talking about? Head to page 175! Get some ideas for a story! Let your imagination go wild! And if you end up writing a story, get a grown-up to help you go online and share it with us at StoryPirates.com.

And now I have a confession to make: I lied. None of that was a huge secret. In fact, it's written right on the back of the book. But I'm a pirate; you can't trust EVERYTHING I say.

THE TOWN OF HILLVIEW had no hills and no view. It was tucked in a valley surrounded by hills, but it was impossible to see them over the enormous stone walls protecting the town, each one fifty feet high. Inside those walls, the grassy ground was as flat as a table. There wasn't a lump, a bump, a gulch, or even a gully to vary the terrain.

Hillview was home to a magical people called the Lysors. But they hadn't always lived there. For centuries, the Lysors had been hailed as protectors of the world. Their ruler, Queen Ailix, had worn a Crystal Crown that gave the Lysors tremendous power. But eleven years ago, everything changed. The Crystal Crown was stolen. The Lysors had to hide. They retreated deep into the valley, built their secret settlement, and walled it off forever. They enchanted the walls so that the entire town vanished into the surrounding landscape like a bird's nest hidden in a pile of twigs.

There was no way in and no way out, and that's how the

Lysors liked it. Inside, they were safe. None of them wanted to see the outside world ever again. None of them, that is, except for Laura. And she had a secret.

On the north end of Hillview was the Never-Dark Forest, where the trees always glowed with a faint green light. It was one of the rare signs of Lysor magic in Hillview, a dim reminder of the power the Lysors once had. The forest grew all the way to the northern wall. Hidden behind the softly glowing leaves of a tall tree was a spot on the wall with three thin cracks, just big enough to see through to the other side. Only Laura knew about it. And it was her favorite place in the entire world. Every day after school, she veered off the path that led to her house and spent hours trying to see what was on the other side of the towering wall.

One pleasantly sunny, utterly windless day, Laura was looking through the cracks in the wall when she spotted a fiery orange fox. Laura stared as it sniffed around the dark soil and pulled a worm out of the ground with its teeth. She tried to sketch as many details as she could in her

notebook, but she knew that the dull gray markings of her pencil could never truly capture the fascinating creature. She pressed her face closer to the stone to try to sear the fox into her memory forever—its inky black eyes, its pointed ears, its white tail so bushy, it looked like it was being followed by a cloud of fur. She didn't even want to breathe for fear of frightening it away.

"Laura!" a loud voice called out from behind her.

Startled, the fox ran away into the hills. Laura sighed, wishing she could do the same. She turned around to see her cousin Millie charging through the trees.

"I've been searching all over for you!" said Millie. "You're going to be late for rations!"

At the beginning of each week, the whole town gathered to collect the food and water that was to last them through the next seven days. Being late was strictly forbidden.

"Already?" Laura said, closing her notebook. She had been staring at the fox for who knows how long.

"Yes!" Millie narrowed her eyes suspiciously. "What are

you doing out here anyway?" She looked behind Laura and gasped. "Are those *cracks* in the wall?!"

"Shh!" said Laura. "It's no big deal. They're barely big enough to look through."

"You were *looking* through them?!" Millie said even louder.

"What's the harm in that?"

"What's the harm?" Millie grabbed Laura's arm. "Anything outside the walls is terrifying!"

Laura sighed. "It was just a little fox eating a worm."

Millie shuddered. "Terrifying and *gross*."

"Just don't tell anyone, okay?"

Millie put her hands on her hips, looking more stern than a twelve-year-old should be capable of looking. "Fine. But if we're late for rations, I'm blaming it on you."

Lara and Millie took off through the Never-Dark Forest, ducking under the glowing branches that blocked their path.

"Hurry!" Millie shouted, her gangly legs kicking behind her so that she looked like a panicked ostrich.

"I'm running as fast as I can!" Laura panted.

They reached the edge of the forest and saw everyone else in Hillview congregated in the center of town. Lysors from dozens of different families lived in Hillview, but they all had one striking resemblance—a lock of glowing green hair, the same green as the trees in the Never-Dark Forest. They were gathered around the Food-Giving Tree, a massive tree with bark the color of chalk. Its branches sagged under the weight of hundreds and hundreds of gray pears, the only fruit that grew in Hillview.

Laura and Millie slipped into the crowd just in time. Laura spotted her dad, Micah, toward the front. Micah was the town healer. He had a friendly, round face, a deep voice, and a silver beard that made him seem older than he was. He tugged nervously at his beard, looking around for Laura.

When he saw her, a relieved smile spread across his face. "There you are! I was worried you were going to be late!"

Laura sidled up next to him. "You worry too much."

Micah chuckled. "You sound just like your mother." He ran his hand through Laura's glowing green lock, which stood out against the rest of her jet-black hair like lightning in the night.

Then a hush fell over the crowd. The sea of Lysors parted as Torian, the mayor of Hillview, walked toward the Food-Giving Tree. He was tall, with wheat-colored hair so thick, it nearly hid the shock of green above his forehead. Like everyone in Hillview, he wore a simple beige tunic over cotton trousers—just thick enough to keep cool in the mildly warm days and warm in the mildly cool nights. Torian was Queen Ailix's brother. When the Crystal Crown was stolen, he led the Lysors in retreat. It was his vision to build the walls, keeping the Lysors hidden—and protected—

forever. But he was a humble man who even disliked the title of mayor. He preferred to go just by his given name, Torian. The only sign of his status was a green pin on his collar shaped like a crescent moon.

"Friends," he addressed the town warmly. "Let's begin."

THE LYSORS SPREAD OUT in a circle around the Food-Giving Tree and held hands. Laura's dad was on her right. On her left was Millie; Millie's mom, Sage; Millie's dad, Simon; and her six younger siblings, Franz, Topher, Mara, Horton, Nadine, and baby Georgie, whose green lock of hair was just a short curl atop his mostly bald head.

Torian began the same speech he gave every Rations Day, which always started with the ancient history of the Lysors. "Thousands of years ago, the great sorceress, Alana, forged the four elements—earth, fire, water, and air—into a Crystal Crown. The Crystal Crown was powerful beyond the strongest mind and could give unlimited power to its user. Alana intended to give the crown to her firstborn child, but then she gave birth to twins—Lysoria, who was virtuous and kind, and Hexia, who was selfish and evil."

The crowd booed at the mention of Hexia's name.

Torian continued, "Lysoria and Hexia fought incessantly over the crown. Alana grew tired of her daughters' sparring and exiled them from the earth, turning each one into a moon. But that didn't stop their descendants, the Lysors and the Hexors, from continuing the fight."

Laura fidgeted impatiently. She had heard this speech so many times, she practically knew it by heart. Millie, on the other hand, was so riveted that she mouthed the words along as Torian spoke.

"After centuries of war, the Lysors won the Crystal Crown once and for all and banished the devious Hexors to a far-off forest. The Hexors were so rotten, they turned the forest putrid. Under Lysor rule, the world had abundant resources and lasting peace." Torian paused for a moment. His voice got quieter. "Then eleven years ago, my sister, Queen Ailix, freed the Hexors from the Putrid Forest. I'll never know why she did it. Perhaps she thought they could change. Instead, they took advantage of her kindness. They stole the crown and took our queen's life."

There was a long silence. Torian wiped a tear from his eye. "But still, we must be thankful. Our great ancestor, Lysoria, shines in the sky each night, her moonlight giving us just enough power to replenish the water in the Endless Well, the fish in the Clear Lake, and the fruit from the Food-Giving Tree. And to keep our precious walls strong so we are safe from our mortal enemies, the Hexors."

The speech had reached its conclusion. Torian joined the circle. Now, it was time for the Lysors to use the limited magic they had left, the magic that had been fading ever since the Crystal Crown was stolen. They squeezed one another's hands tightly and closed their eyes.

All at once, they whispered the ancient Lysorian word for water: "Oighar'e."

If Laura's eyes had been open, she would have seen that for a moment, the green locks of hair and the trees in the Never-Dark Forest glowed as brightly as galaxies in a night sky. Behind her, the Endless Well filled with water. Across the town, the Clear Lake teemed with fish.

Then the Lysors spoke the word used to harness the power of the earth: "Talamh'e."

Laura heard a familiar sound, like it was raining rocks.

Thud! Thud-thud! Thud-thud-thud!

When the noise finally stopped, the Lysors let go of one another's hands and opened their eyes to see the ground covered in ripe gray pears, freshly fallen from the tree. The branches were now covered in colorless gray pear blossoms that would grow into new fruit by the following week.

Torian clapped his hands. "Who's ready for gray pears?!"

The whole town let out a thunderous cheer, Millie loudest of all. Laura sighed and began filling her rucksack with the mushy, flavorless fruit. Even though she despised each bite of gray pear more than the last, she had to collect as many as she could. By the end of the week, there wouldn't be much else to eat.

While the Lysor children stayed to collect gray pears, the elder Lysors went to fetch the rest of the rations—two jugs of water from the Endless Well, three fish from the Clear Lake, and a sack of grain. And that was it for the whole week.

Micah hoisted up the handles of his wooden wheelbarrow.

"See you at home," he said to Laura. Grinning, he added, "Don't eat all the gray pears."

"Very funny, Dad," said Laura, throwing another pear in her sack. "Almost as funny as when you said it last week."

As Micah pushed the wheelbarrow toward the Endless Well, Laura called after him, "And the week before that!"

The sound of boisterous laughter and chatter filled the air as the kids ran around the Food-Giving Tree, snatching up pears as quickly as they could. Rations Day was special—it broke up the monotony of Hillview. It was the only way to tell one week from the next, like starting a new chapter in a book, even though every page had the same words on it.

Millie stuffed gray pears into her rucksack while trying to keep an eye on all her siblings. As the oldest child in the biggest family in Hillview, it always fell to her to ensure they had enough food. "Horton, stop kicking it! That's your dinner!" she called to her five-year-old brother. She swatted her little sister Mara's arm. "Don't eat it now, you'll spoil your appetite!" she scolded. "We're having gray pear pie tonight!"

Laura watched Millie chase frantically after her siblings as if she were trying to catch a dozen butterflies at once. Sometimes Laura wished she had a brother or sister of her own, but never on Rations Day. She spotted baby Georgie toddling away from Millie. He was reaching out for a gray pear, when a mud-caked boot stomped down, squashing it to bits. The boot belonged to Claude, a blockheaded boy Laura knew from school.

"Too slow!" said Claude with a shrill laugh.

Georgie burst into tears.

Laura ran over and scooped up Georgie in her arms. She scowled at Claude. "Why would you smash a little kid's gray pear?"

"Sorry, did *you* want to eat it?" he said in a syrupy voice. "You can scrape it off my boot if you want."

Laura narrowed her eyes. "I'd rather eat my own tongue."

Claude smirked. "I saw you were almost late today. Were you out looking for adventure?" he said mockingly.

"Actually, I was out looking for your brain."

Laura and Claude had never gotten along. In school, she was known for asking too many questions, which annoyed Claude to no end. Especially because he was the kind of person who never had any answers.

Claude's eyes flickered to the notebook tucked under Laura's arm. "What's that?" he asked.

Before she could answer, he reached out his meaty hand and snatched it away.

Laura set Georgie down in the grass. "Give that back!" she snapped.

Claude held it high over her head. "Why? Is it your *diary*?" He snickered. "Dear Diary, my name is Laura, and I don't have any friends."

Millie waddled over, her heavy sack of pears straining her shoulder. "She does have a friend! And her name is me!"

Claude burst out laughing. "I said *friends. Plurals.*"

"It's plural, you dead-eyed fish carcass!" Laura lunged at him, reaching for the notebook, but he pulled it away.

"Let's see what's in here." He flipped through the pages until he got to the drawing of the fox. He ripped it out of the notebook and eyed it suspiciously. "Did you make this up?"

"No. I saw it," Laura said firmly.

Claude scoffed. "Where?"

"Yes, where?" said a voice behind them. It was Torian. He plucked the paper from Claude's hand.

Laura froze. Millie let out a high-pitched squeak.

Torian studied the drawing, a perplexed look on his face. He read Laura's notes aloud in a soft voice. "Eyes like black pebbles. Fur the color of autumn. Sharp teeth."

By now, the kids had stopped collecting gray pears and were all staring at Laura. The older Lysors were coming back to the tree, wheelbarrows half-full, to see what was going on.

Torian locked eyes with Laura. "Where did you see this creature?"

Laura looked away, not wanting to give up her secret.

Torian put his hand on Laura's shoulder. "You can tell me."

She took a deep breath. "Outside the walls."

A gasp rippled through the crowd.

Torian's voice remained calm. "How?"

Laura's eyes darted back and forth. She saw her dad standing nearby, his brow furrowed with worry. She didn't know what else to say except the truth. It all came spilling out like water from the Endless Well. "There are cracks in the wall. Near my house. Past the Never-Dark Forest."

There were more gasps from the crowd and cries of surprise.

Laura continued, "It's only a few slivers, just big enough to peek through."

"And you were there today?" Torian asked.

Laura nodded. "I go there whenever I miss my mom." She paused. "Every day."

Torian squeezed her shoulder, his deep brown eyes filled with kindness. "I understand." He turned to the crowd and raised his voice so everyone could hear. "But any glimpse of the outside world will only lead to peril!" He held up the drawing and pointed to the fox. "What lies beyond the walls is far more dangerous than this!"

An elder Lysor raised his walking stick and shouted, "Hear, hear!"

Torian's voice grew more passionate by the word. "We all

know the Hexors have the Crystal Crown. Their power has never been stronger. They are horrible monsters who will stop at nothing to destroy us. In here, we are protected." He stretched out his hands. "When we work together—*all* of us—we can remain safe forever!"

The crowd burst into excited applause.

Torian shouted above the din, "Promise us, Laura! Promise us you'll never look outside the walls again!"

Laura took in the expectant faces surrounding her. Millie, wide-eyed; her dad, tugging at his beard. With a taste in her mouth more awful than any gray pear she'd ever eaten, she softly said, "I promise."

"LOOK AT THAT ONE!" Millie said, pointing up at a cloud in the sky.

She and Laura lay side by side in the grass at the edge of the Never-Dark Forest. It had been five days since Laura had made her promise, and she had managed to steer clear of the cracks in the wall. But it wasn't easy. All week, she felt as though she had a giant itch that she wasn't allowed to scratch. It made her intolerably grumpy. So Millie had invented a game to cheer her up. They would stare up at the sky and take turns naming what each passing cloud looked like. Millie had strained her imagination as hard as she could to come up with the name of the game. It was called "What's That Cloud?"

Laura examined the puffy white shape overhead. "I think it looks like a one-eyed bear," she said. "That's twenty feet tall! And shoots fire out of its ears!"

Millie covered her mouth to keep from screaming. "That's horrifying!"

Laura laughed. "Well, what do you think it looks like?"

Millie smiled. "I think it looks like a gray pear."

Laura elbowed her lightly in the arm. "That's what you say for every one."

"It's not my fault all the clouds look delicious!"

"Fine," Laura said, pointing at Millie. "But you have to come up with something new next time."

Laura turned to face the sky again. She had to admit to herself that she liked the game. Without the cracks in the wall, the clouds drifting overhead were the only glimpse she had left of the outside world.

"I'll try," said Millie. "I just don't know where you get these wild ideas."

Laura shrugged. "My dad has told me all sorts of stories about what life was like before the Lysors fled to Hillview. There are creatures out there unlike anything we've ever seen! Wolves with big teeth that howl at the moons all night . . ."

Millie raised her eyebrows. "Yeah, right."

"And fish so big, you could eat one for a whole week!"

"You're joking."

"I'm not!" said Laura. "And there are dragons!"

"Okay, that's enough!" Millie stuck her fingers in her ears. "This conversation was fun until it wasn't!"

"Come on, don't you have to tell bedtime stories to Horton and Nadine? This is good material."

"Yeah, but those stories are supposed to put them to *sleep*, not keep them up all night in terror!"

Laura pointed up at a cluster of clouds. "What do you think those look like? Use your imagination. Think outside the walls."

"Okay . . ." Millie furrowed her brow and mashed her lips together in concentration. "It's . . . a . . . cat?"

Laura nodded encouragingly. "Yeah . . ."

"With a long tail . . ."

"Go on. . . ."

"Eating a bushel of gray pears!"

Laura smacked her forehead and collapsed onto the grass. "You're impossible." She shielded her eyes against the bright sun. "Be honest. Haven't you ever wanted to go beyond the walls? Aren't you at least a tiny bit curious?"

Millie shifted uneasily. "Curious? Maybe. But you could be curious about what the bottom of the Endless Well looks like, that doesn't mean you should dive in." She rolled onto her side to face Laura. "My parents have told me stories, too. What about Queen Ailix? There were no walls protecting her, and look what happened."

Laura leaped to her feet. "So just because something terrible happened when we were babies, we have to be trapped in Hillview for the rest of our lives?"

Millie sighed. "We're not trapped."

"Well, we can't get out. That sounds like trapped to me."

"You're looking at it all wrong. Sure, we can't get out, but nothing else can get *in*! Without the Crystal Crown, Lysors can't protect the world. What else can we do but protect ourselves? Our power is fading every day. The Never-Dark Forest is getting dimmer. And what about our hair?" Millie said, clutching her green lock. "Don't you remember when we were little, it used to be so bright, it would keep you up at night?"

"Yeah, but—"

"The Hexors have the crown, and that means they have all the power, and *that* means the world is getting more and more dangerous by the minute. You'd have to be out of your mind to go outside the walls—it's a death wish!"

Laura flinched. Grief struck her like a punch to the gut.

Millie saw that she had said the wrong thing. She stood up quickly. "I—I'm sorry. I didn't mean—" She fumbled for words. "I wasn't talking about your mom."

"I know." Laura looked at the massive gray walls, then turned back to Millie. "I guess—I just want to be able to see what she saw." She nudged Millie's shoulder and smiled, trying to lighten the mood. "I mean, come on! It's called Hillview, and we don't even have a view of any hills!"

Millie's eyes narrowed in determination. She turned her back to Laura and crouched down. "Get on my shoulders."

"What?!"

"You heard me. Get on my shoulders."

"You're nuts."

"Have you seen how many gray pears I can carry?" She patted her shoulders. "Hop up!"

"Okay . . . ," Laura said tentatively. She awkwardly climbed up onto Millie's shoulders.

With a hearty grunt, Millie straightened her legs, standing up tall. "What do you see?"

Laura looked around. "Uh . . ."

"Quick, Laura!" Millie groaned. "This is actually way more painful than I thought it would be."

Laura craned her neck to see as high as she could. Over the top of the farthest wall she could just make out a slice of green hilltop peppered with pine trees. "I see it! It's a view! Of a hill!"

And with that, Millie collapsed to the ground, sending Laura rolling onto the grass. They both burst into hysterical laughter.

When Laura was finally able to catch her breath, she looked over at Millie and smiled. "Thanks."

"Anytime." Millie rubbed her shoulder. "Well, not *any* time. But, occasionally." She noticed the sun creeping down toward the west wall. She gasped. "I've got to get home! I have to start making the Thew for tonight."

Laura felt a little queasy at the mention of the Thew. It was one of Millie's signature dishes. Near the end of the week as the rations were growing thin, it was important to use every last scrap of food. The Thew was a thick mixture of ground fish bones, soggy oats, and gray pear seeds that had been soaked overnight and mashed into a paste. Laura had tried it once. It tasted like a foot.

"The Thew? Already?" Laura asked.

"It has to simmer for six hours, and if I don't stir it constantly, it starts to develop a skin."

Laura shuddered. "Don't save me any."

Millie snorted. "Have you seen how much my brothers eat? I'll be lucky if I get any myself!"

Millie dashed off, and Laura headed down the dirt path toward her home. She walked past the schoolhouse and into the Never-Dark Forest. She stopped to look at the leaves on the trees. Millie was right. They were getting dimmer. But their magical glow still filled Laura with a sense of wonder. As the path led her closer to the cracks in the walls, she found herself slowing down. They drew her in like a magnet. As was often the case when Laura was forbidden from doing something, she found it all the more enticing. The itch she couldn't scratch grew almost unbearable. It wasn't just curiosity that tempted her to look. It was a longing deep in her bones.

Laura's mom, Reina, had been an explorer. She'd spent her life traveling the world, facing the unknown, seeing what no one else had seen before. Laura had only one memory of her mom, from when she was just a baby. Reina was lifting her up in the air. Laura must have been barely a year old, but she could still remember that feeling, like she was flying.

Laura's biggest dream was to be an explorer. Even if all she could explore was the small patch of ground visible through the cracks in the wall, it was the closest she ever felt to her mom.

Against her better judgment, she took a step closer to the wall. What was on the other side right now? Another fox? Once she had seen a deer with antlers so big, it looked like tree branches were growing out of its head, but that was years ago. Even just a glimpse might scratch the itch.

She knew she had made a promise to Torian, but would it really matter if she took one little peek? She checked to make sure no one was around. She was totally alone. She couldn't resist. She sprinted to the wall and pressed her face to the cracks.

At first, she didn't see much of anything. Then, she spotted something flying through the air. For a moment, she thought it was a strange bird. But as it got closer, she saw that it was a gleaming silver arrow with violet feathers on the end—and it was soaring straight toward the wall.

The arrow pierced the stone with a loud *thwunk!*

Hillview was under attack.

LAURA TORE OUT OF the forest so fast that her feet kicked up tiny explosions in the dirt. She ran through the center of Hillview, past the Endless Well and the Food-Giving Tree until she reached Torian's house at the edge of the south wall. Just like all the other homes in town, it was a white stone structure with a thatched roof made of straw and reeds.

Laura banged on the door as hard as she could. *"Torian!"* she shouted. "Come quick!"

Some Lysor kids playing nearby in the Clear Lake stopped what they were doing and wandered over to see what the commotion was about.

Laura pounded on the door so hard, she thought it might fall off its hinges. "Hello?! Anybody in there?!"

The door flung open, and Torian stepped outside. "Laura," he said with surprise. "Is everything all right?"

"No, everything is *not* all right," she said, panting.

Several Lysors started to gather in front of Torian's house, their faces a mixture of curiosity and concern.

He gave them a small, reassuring wave, then turned back to Laura. "Well, what's wrong?"

"Someone's attacking the town!" she exploded.

Torian's face twisted in confusion. "That's impossible. The enchantment makes Hillview completely invisible to the outside eye."

"Well, someone found it. I don't know how, but it's true," Laura insisted. "Follow me!" She turned and started running back toward the Never-Dark Forest.

Torian hurried behind her, along with the group of Lysors who had gathered in front of his house. As they made their way through the town, more Lysors darted out of their homes and joined the group. Millie came outside wearing an apron covered in fish-bone dust and holding a wooden spoon. She recognized something she rarely saw on Laura's face—fear. She dropped the spoon and ran after her.

Micah was in his study when he glanced out the window and saw Laura leading a parade of panic that was growing larger by the minute.

He raced outside. "Laura! What's going on?"

Without breaking her stride, she shouted, "I saw an arrow hit the outside of the wall!"

A flash of exasperation crossed Micah's face. "You were looking through the cracks again?"

"You can ground me later, Dad! Come on!"

By the time Laura reached the forest, the entire town was following behind her. She led them to the spot that until then she had never shown anyone.

"There," she said, pointing to the cracks. "Someone shot an arrow at the wall. Look!"

Half the Lysors were practically climbing over each other to get close, while the other half hung back in fear.

Torian turned to the crowd, his back against the wall. "Please remain calm. I will get to the bottom of this."

He pressed his face to the cracks for what felt like an eternity. Then he turned around and looked at Laura as if she were a puzzle he couldn't solve. A very frustrating puzzle. That was missing too many pieces. "There's nothing there," he said.

"What?!" said Laura, her stomach twisting as if she'd just eaten a bowlful of Millie's Thew. She rushed to the wall and looked for herself. Sure enough, the silver arrow was gone. "I—I swear I saw it," she stammered.

Torian addressed the Lysors. "My friends, there is no arrow. We are not under attack. This was all"—he shot Laura a look—"a misunderstanding."

A wave of relief washed over the crowd, then just as quickly, the tide turned to anger. The Lysors' eyes sharpened into daggers, and they erupted in shouts of outrage.

"Well then, what is the meaning of this?!"

"The girl is nothing but trouble!"

"I knew she was a liar," said Claude, smacking his older brother, Melvin, on the back. "You owe me a gray pear!"

Laura tried to meet her dad's eyes, but his hand was covering his face. Still, though, she could see his disappointment.

"I'm telling the truth!" Laura insisted.

This only seemed to anger the crowd more.

"Friends," Torian said, raising his voice above the din. "Don't judge too harshly. It's not the Lysor way. After all, Laura is only a child, and we all know children tend to imagine things."

Laura bristled. "I didn't imagine—"

Torian spoke over her. "Now we've seen what happens when our eyes wander outside. Fear! Confusion! Chaos! The solution is as clear as our precious lake. We must seal up these cracks immediately!"

The crowd roared with approval.

"This isn't about the cracks in the wall!" Laura shouted in desperation. "There's something out there!"

"What's out there doesn't concern us. All that matters is what's in here," said Torian. "We must seal the cracks!"

The crowd roared even louder.

Laura exploded, "Do you have gray pears for brains?! This isn't going to solve anything!"

Micah pushed through the crowd and grabbed her shoulders. "Laura, stop! Please!"

She looked up at his face. "You believe me, don't you, Dad?"

He sighed heavily, searching for the right words. "I . . . think . . . sometimes you want an adventure so badly that your imagination gets away from you."

Suddenly Laura felt completely and utterly alone. Which is an especially terrible feeling in a crowd.

The Lysors began to chant, "The walls will never fall! The walls will never fall!"

Torian picked up a handful of dirt and spread it over the cracked wall.

"Talamh'e," he uttered, and the dirt turned to stone.

Laura watched as the last light from the outside world disappeared. Her mind hovered somewhere between fury and devastation, when she felt a hand on her shoulder. It was Millie. Laura turned to her, red-eyed.

"I believe you," Millie said.

"My friends," said Torian, "we are safer today than we were yesterday." He raised his fist and shouted triumphantly, "The walls will never fall!"

Boom!

The earth shook violently, and the entire north wall crumbled to the ground.

THE FIRST THING LAURA saw was a shock of violet hair glowing through the dust of the fallen wall. And then another. The quake had knocked the Lysors to the ground, and they covered their heads in terror. Two Hexors, a man and a woman, galloped through the wreckage on horseback. The woman wore a gleaming wolf pelt around her shoulders. Her short blond hair looked as if it had been chopped with a dull blade. She carried a bow in her right hand, and strapped to her shoulder was a quiver with a single arrow in it. Silver. With violet feathers.

The man wore a mangy cloak of weasel pelts roughly stitched together. He was so big and broad that he made his enormous horse look like a pony. His thick arms were so hairy that it was hard to tell where his fur cloak ended and his arms began.

As they circled around the Lysors, Laura saw that the horses they rode had no eyes.

The woman surveyed the area, then smiled broadly. Her teeth were as black as tar. "So this is it. The lost Lysor city. I'll admit, using your powers to make it invisible was pretty clever. I've been scouring this valley for years." She pulled the silver arrow from her quiver. "But an enchanted Hexor arrow will always break a Lysorian spell." She turned to the man. "What do you think of this place, Hugo?"

Hugo looked around the Never-Dark Forest and scratched his bulbous chin. He grinned, revealing his own black teeth. "Well, Erika. I think it's pretty crummy."

Erika nodded. "Eleven years looking for *this*?" She spat onto the ground. The grass where the glob of black saliva landed instantly withered and died. "Where's Queen Ailix?" she demanded.

Torian pulled himself to his feet. Erika quickly loaded the silver arrow into her bow and pointed it straight at his heart. "Move another inch and it'll be your last."

Torian froze. "Queen Ailix is dead," he said, his voice shaking.

"Huh." Erika glanced at Hugo. "This day gets better and better." She turned back to Torian. "Well, unless you want to meet the same fate as your queen, I suggest you hand over the Crystal Crown."

"*Strongly* suggest!" Hugo added, gnawing on his yellow fingernail.

Beads of sweat gathered on Torian's forehead. "We—"

He tried to steady his voice. "We don't have the Crystal Crown. You Hexors stole it."

"Liar!" Erika snarled, pulling back her arrow. "We Hexors have been searching for the crown ever since we were able to escape the Putrid Forest. You think you can trick me into believing one of our own has had it this whole time? What kind of fools do you think we are?"

"Ow!" Hugo cried.

Erika whipped her head around. "What is it?"

"I accidentally bit off my whole fingernail."

Erika sighed, rubbing her temples. "Enough of this nonsense. Hugo, search the houses! Turn this place upside down!"

Hugo looked at her, confused. "I don't think I'm that strong."

"Just go, you drooling oaf!"

"Yes, ma'am!" He spurred his horse and it galloped off toward the Lysor homes.

Erika spoke with contempt. "Nobody move, or I'll strike you all down. Believe me, I'd love an excuse to wipe out all the Lysors at once."

From the middle of the crowd, Claude snorted. "You only have one arrow."

Erika narrowed her eyes at him. "One *enchanted* arrow." She aimed at a nearby tree and let the arrow fly. It punctured the thick trunk. The glowing green leaves turned violet and began to wither.

Erika beckoned to the arrow, and it reversed course, flying straight back toward her.

Laura realized that was how the arrow had disappeared from the wall.

Erika loaded the arrow back into the bow. "One arrow is all I need."

Claude gulped loudly.

In the distance, Laura saw Hugo ransacking the houses one by one—including her own. He didn't even bother to get off his horse before entering with reckless abandon. There was an ongoing racket of glass breaking, pots clambering, and heavy wooden furniture being flipped over.

Laura huddled between her dad and Millie, who was trembling in fear.

"We have to do something," Laura whispered. "The Crystal Crown isn't here."

Millie let out a soft squeak. "When that guy comes back empty-handed, we're going to be skewered like fish kebabs!"

"Keep calm," said Micah. "Torian will figure out a solution."

All three of them looked over at Torian, who stared petrified at the arrow pointed at his chest.

Micah grimaced. "I hope."

Hugo emerged from a house, shouting in frustration. "I can't find it!"

"It's here somewhere," Erika called to him. "It has to be. Keep looking."

Hugo galloped along the path and into the next house—Millie's.

Millie winced. "I hope that horse is housebroken."

They heard Hugo clanging around inside.

Millie clasped her hands together. "Please don't spill the Thew. It took me all day to make it."

Micah's eyes went wide. He whispered, "Millie, is the Thew still on the fire?"

Millie nodded. "It needs at least another hour before the broth soaks up all the fish-bone flavor."

A look of determination that Laura had never seen before crossed Micah's face. A change had come over her father.

"What are you doing?" Laura asked.

"Something I haven't done in a very long time." He closed his eyes. His lock of hair blazed green. The trees around him glowed brighter. He whispered an ancient Lysor word. "Tier'e."

Fire.

There was a loud *pop!* and a flash of light from inside Millie's house, followed by a shriek of pain. The horse galloped out of the house, neighing in alarm. Hugo staggered out after it, covered in smoldering Thew.

"Aaagh! It's so hot!" he wailed, stumbling around the front yard. "I don't know what happened. The fire just . . . exploded!"

Erika's eyes darted in confusion from Hugo to the Lysors. "Which one of you did this?" she shouted. "Tell me!"

Micah stepped forward. "I did."

"Dad, no!" Laura whimpered. She didn't understand. Why was he doing this?

Erika pointed the arrow at him. She drew it back so far it looked like the bowstring might snap. "How?"

Micah looked her in the eye. "Lysor magic may be weak, but it's far from dead."

"We'll see about that." She released the silver arrow. It soared through the air.

Just as it was about to hit Micah in the neck, he uttered, "Goith'e."

Wind.

A colossal wind blew through the forest, scooping the arrow up in its invisible arms and carrying it all the way to the Clear Lake. There was a soft splash as it landed in the water.

Erika laughed sharply. "Nice try."

She reached out to beckon for the arrow. But before she could move her fingers, Micah bellowed, "Oighar'e!"

Water.

The Clear Lake froze over, as if a thousand winters had descended in a single second. The arrow was trapped beneath the ice. Erika let out a bloodcurdling cry of anger.

Exhausted, Micah collapsed to the ground.

"Dad!" Laura cried, wrapping her arms around him.

"I'll be okay," he said weakly.

"This isn't over!" Erika shouted. "In fact, it's just the beginning. Hugo, get over here!"

Hugo was galumphing around Millie's front yard, chasing his nervous horse and rubbing his wounds. "Coming!"

He managed to clumsily climb onto the horse and rode over to Erika. A gruesome red blister was raised on his forearm where the Thew had burned it.

Erika continued, "Now that I've found the lost Lysor city, I'll return with the entire Hexor army. Unless you hand over the Crystal Crown, we'll destroy this place along with every last Lysor!" She smiled, her teeth as black as death. "Don't miss me too much."

She laughed as she galloped over the wreckage of the wall and into the hills. Hugo started after her.

"Wait," said Micah. He dragged himself to his feet and approached Hugo carefully. "This will help with the burn." He pulled out a single strand of his green hair and wrapped it around the blister on Hugo's arm. Immediately, the redness died down and the wound began to heal.

Surprised, Hugo looked for a moment as though he was about to thank Micah. Instead, he yanked his arm away and scowled. "You have two days." He rode off into the dim evening light.

As soon as the Hexors were out of sight, the Lysors

turned to each other in panic. Their homes were wrecked. The north wall was a pile of rubble.

An elder Lysor called out, "If the Hexors don't have the crown, who does?"

Torian looked as confused as anyone. "I—I have no idea."

Millie pulled her brothers and sisters close, trying to comfort them. "The Hexor army will be here in two days!" she called out. "What are we going to do? We have to run! We have to hide!"

Laura looked at Torian. He was so pale, she thought he might faint. But as he dabbed the sweat from his forehead, she saw his expression transform in an instant, as if he were putting on a mask of confidence.

"There is nowhere else to hide," he said. "There is only one solution. We rebuild!" He turned to Micah. "Thank you for your bravery. Laura, take your father home so he can replenish his strength." He turned back to the crowd. "The rest of you—our work begins now! By dawn, we'll have a new wall, even bigger and stronger than before, and no one will come in again!"

"DAD, THAT WAS INCREDIBLE!" Laura said, handing Micah a cup of warm oat tea. He was lying in bed, looking twenty years older than he had an hour earlier. Fighting off the Hexors had really taken a toll.

He managed a weak smile. "Pretty impressive, right?"

"*Pretty* impressive? You fought off that Hexor with a Thew bomb—kaboom!" She leaped across the room. "You trapped an enchanted arrow in the lake—and then you froze the whole lake!" She shook her head in amazement. "I had no idea you could do all that!"

Micah chuckled. "Your old dad's still got some tricks up his sleeve. I can dance, too." He started wiggling like an awkward worm.

Laura held up her hand and laughed. "Okay, too far." She looked around at the mess Hugo had made. A heavy chest of drawers was tipped onto its side. The kitchen cabinets were torn off their hinges. There were hoof marks and smashed gray pears all over the floor. Laura sighed. "This is why you should never ride a horse indoors."

She picked up Micah's clothes from the floor and folded them in a neat pile.

"Laura, I need to tell you something," Micah said, straining to sit up in bed. "I should have believed you when you said that Hillview was under attack. You don't have an overactive imagination. You're brave enough to see the truth when others are afraid to look. I'm sorry."

Laura sat down on the edge of the bed. "It's okay, Dad."

He took her hand. "You're my daughter and I trust you. Go to the cabinet in my study. It's time you learned there's more to Lysor magic than growing gray pears."

Her eyes lit up. She had never been allowed to open the cabinet in her dad's study. She raced to the cabinet and found a box with a crescent moon etched on the lid. She brought it to Micah.

"When the Lysors had the Crystal Crown, the world thrived with life," he said. "Rushing rivers, bountiful crops, wildflowers so vibrant, it looked like all the beauty of a sunset had sprouted from a tiny seed."

Laura smiled at the thought. The only flowers that grew in Hillview were dull gray pear blossoms.

"There was no limit to what we could do. And I was a great healer."

"You still are," said Laura.

"Not like I used to be." Micah opened the box, revealing

glass bottles of strangely colored liquids. The labels were written in ancient Lysorian that Laura couldn't understand. "This is all that's left of my healing tonics." He picked up a bottle that contained a little bit of pale orange liquid. "This one replenishes energy, even when it's dangerously low."

Laura looked at her dad's weary face. "Why don't you take some now?"

Micah shook his head. "I won't use any of these for myself. They're down to the last drops. Lysor magic is too weak for me to make more. So I save them for when they are most needed."

"Why did you waste your magic healing that horrible Hexor?" Laura asked.

He looked her in the eye and placed his hand on her arm. "Everyone deserves to be healed. Lysor or Hexor, it doesn't matter. Always remember that." He turned his attention back to the bottles. "This one is for a cold—amazing how something so common can be so difficult to cure."

Laura picked up a small bottle that appeared to have nothing inside. "Why do you have this empty one?

"It isn't empty," said Micah. "That's Chamelixir. It makes you blend into your surroundings. Of course, the Chamelixir also blends into *its* surroundings, which is why you can't see it."

Laura started to put it back in the box.

"Keep it," said Micah.

Laura was stunned. In Hillview, Lysor children were

allowed to use magic only to help replenish the resources on Rations Day. Elder Lysors were supposed to restrict their own use of magic as much as possible. It was the only way to make their limited power last.

"Are you sure?" she asked.

Micah nodded. "Laura, if the walls fall again, you need to be able to hide yourself. I don't know how much is left in there, but you only need a drop. And remember—after you take it, don't use any other magic, or the effects will reverse immediately."

Laura placed the bottle of Chamelixir in her pocket. She really hoped she wouldn't have to use it. "What are we going to do when the Hexors come back?" she asked, dread rising in her voice.

He put his hand on hers, trying to comfort her. "Hopefully the wall will be strong enough by then to keep them out."

"That's not enough!"

His eyes crinkled in concern. "Maybe not. But we have to try."

Laura jumped up from the bed, exasperated. She stormed over to the wooden chest that had been toppled over in the corner. Its contents were spilled out on the floor.

She heard Torian's voice in her head: *We rebuild!*

How could the entire town think that would work? Two Hexors had gotten past the wall as if it were nothing. A whole army would blast it to dust. She pushed the chest upright and roughly stuffed the items back inside—an old sweater dotted with moth holes; a wristwatch that had stopped working long ago—then she picked up something that caught her eye. A notebook with a worn leather cover. She riffled through the pages, which were filled with writing and sketches. The paper was thick and pulpy, as though it had been pressed by hand.

"Dad, what is this?"

He squinted at it. A smile of recognition came over his face. "Oh. I haven't looked at that in years. It's your mother's notes from when she was out exploring."

Laura gasped. "Mom wrote all this?" She looked at the pages more closely now, tracing her finger along the lines of writing.

"She always took detailed notes during her travels. Then when she returned, she would report back to Queen Ailix. Because of your mother, the queen knew when crops were dying or rivers were drying up. Then, with a flash of the Crystal Crown, Queen Ailix would make things right again. Who knows how many lives your mother saved with her adventurous spirit."

Laura's heart swelled with pride.

Micah's gaze drifted out the window. "But that adventurous spirit is also why we lost her." He tugged at his beard. "The last time she left, she didn't want to go. But the Crystal Crown had just been stolen, and . . . I've never told you this, but . . . your mother went to find it."

Laura's mouth dropped open. "Really?"

"You were just a baby. She was heartbroken to leave you. But she was even more terrified of the world you would have to live in if the Lysors didn't have the crown." He paused. "But she never found it. And she never came home. And we had no choice but to flee to Hillview."

Laura had so many questions that it was hard to choose where to begin. "If Mom never came back, how do you have her notebook?"

"A clever trick she came up with," Micah said. "Your mother never had much interest in Lysor magic, but she could be pretty good at it when she tried. Let me show you." He pulled himself out of bed with a groan and shuffled over to his desk. He opened the bottom drawer. "It must be in here somewhere," he mumbled. "Ah, found it!" He pulled out a stack of parchment paper and set it on the desk and explained, "This paper was made from a tree in the Never-Dark Forest. Your mother enchanted it so that whatever she wrote on it also appeared in that notebook. Bring it here."

Laura brought over the notebook. Micah opened it to a clean page. Then he took a sheet of parchment from the top of the stack. He wrote, *Hi, Laura. Please make me some more oat tea.* As he wrote on the parchment, the ink glowed green and the same words appeared on the blank notebook page in his handwriting.

Laura laughed. "That's amazing!"

"Your mother was an amazing person. I always worried

about her when she was away, so she left me this notebook. She would take a stack of the parchment and write to me as often as she could. If she was climbing an ice-covered mountain or flying around on a unicorn, I could see it all through her eyes."

Laura looked at him skeptically. "A unicorn? Seriously?"

"Seriously!" Micah turned to a page with a rough sketch of a unicorn surrounded by detailed notes. It reminded Laura of her sketch of the orange fox.

"You mother's calling was to explore the world, while mine was to stay with the Lysors. And with you, of course. Through this notebook, I knew she was safe. Then one day, she stopped writing." His voice cracked a little. "That's how I knew she was gone."

Laura put her head on her dad's shoulder. "Why don't you get back in bed. I'll make you some more tea."

Micah closed the notebook and handed it to her. "Here. It's yours."

THAT NIGHT, LAURA STAYED up for hours poring over the notebook. Through her window, she could see the two moons that rose in the sky each evening. The moon of Hexia shone a bright violet, while Lysoria glowed green. Their light served as a reminder of the two sisters who were banished to the sky long ago, the ancestors of the Lysors and the Hexors.

Laura read through the notebook by candlelight. She turned the pages slowly, savoring each line. She felt as if she were meeting her mother for the first time. Once, Reina had fallen into a rushing river that carried her for miles before she was able to grasp a tree root—but then the root turned out to be a snake! Another time, she had climbed a sheer rock face, but when she got to the top, the summit was covered in fire ants, and she'd had to climb all the way back down. Every page was filled with the kind of adventure Laura could only ever dream of having from within the walls. Some pages had detailed drawings and bizarre descriptions, while others had snippets of thoughts—the smell of a winter's first snow, the prickliness of a pine cone.

Laura was struck not only by her mother's bravery but also by her playfulness. Next to a sketch of a mammoth, she had written to Micah, "Found your twin!"

Laura laughed out loud. The mammoth, with its woolly face, did look remarkably like her dad.

Laura realized that the unscratchable itch she'd always felt wasn't just because she was confined within the walls of Hillview. It was because she was her mother's daughter. That longing to explore was as much a part of her as her shock of green hair.

After hours of reading, a pit started to form in Laura's stomach. She knew that soon she would reach the final page. Her dread slowed her down, but her curiosity compelled her to keep reading. Finally, as the moons were starting to set in the sky, she reached the end of the writing. The rest of the pages were blank. Sadness crushed Laura like a heavy stone. This was all she would ever know of her mom.

She blew out the candle. The only light in the room came from the moons. Laura was about to close the notebook when Lysoria shifted ever so slightly in the sky, casting a dim green light onto the blank page. And where the light hit, Laura saw that there was one more sentence. The ink was so faint, she could hardly see it. It seemed to be revealed only by the light of Lysoria. She held the notebook closer to the window. As the ink soaked up the light, it became just bright enough for Laura to read. When she saw what it said, her heart started thumping so fast, it felt as if a jackrabbit were trapped in her chest.

Bloato wears the Crystal Crown.

Laura couldn't believe it. If this was true, then not all hope was lost. Hiding away forever wasn't the only solution.

Laura flipped through the rest of the notebook, holding it under Lysoria's waning light. There were no more hidden messages. All she had to go on was one sentence. She had no idea who—or what—Bloato was, but it was a start. If she could find the Crystal Crown and bring it back, she could save Hillview and the Lysors once and for all.

But if she was going to do it, she had to leave immediately. It was almost dawn. The Lysors had been working through the night to rebuild the north wall. Soon, her only chance of escape would be sealed up—if it wasn't already. She didn't have any time to think. She hurriedly filled her rucksack with some clothes, a blanket, and a few scraps of food.

She tiptoed into Micah's room. His face was pressed into a pillow, and he was snoring loudly. She placed her mother's notebook on his desk, then grabbed the stack of enchanted parchment. As she wrote on the parchment, the ink glowed green and her words appeared in the notebook. "I'm going to get the Crystal Crown. I'll be back soon." Then she added, "Don't eat all the gray pears."

She shoved the pile of parchment into her rucksack and slipped out into the cool morning air.

The Never-Dark Forest was teeming with Lysors reconstructing the north wall. Some pushed wheelbarrows heavy with rocks, others teetered on tall ladders, laying the stones with a cement made of pulverized gray pears. By now, much of the wall was as tall as it had been before the Hexors arrived, though a few sections were still unfinished. The wall looked a little like a giant mouth that was missing a few teeth.

Laura darted between the trees, her mind racing nearly as quickly as her feet. She had to find a way out before the wall was complete. She noticed a section that was lower than the rest, but it was still too tall for her to make it over. Then she spotted the tree. Its glowing branches grew just close enough to the low section of the wall. If Laura was bold enough to climb it, she just might be able to jump.

There was one Lysor working nearby. Laura waited silently for him to lift the last heavy stone out of his wheelbarrow and place it on the wall. As soon as he left to refill the wheelbarrow, Laura knew it was her chance.

She raced to the tree and pulled herself up onto the lowest branch, the rough bark scraping her palms. As she scrambled higher, the strap of her rucksack got caught on a twig, but she wrenched it free. She reached the branch that was level with the top of the wall. She edged out as far as she could until the bough began to sag under her weight.

With the thought of the Crystal Crown clear in her mind, she leaped through the air and caught the edge of the wall. She pulled herself up, and for the first time in her life, she had a full view of the hills stretching out into the distance. She took a moment to marvel at the bright morning sunlight hitting the tops of the pine trees. Some part of her was afraid. But mostly she was so thrilled, it almost made her dizzy. She felt as if she had spent her whole life looking at shadows, and now she could finally see light. She was about to swing her legs over the wall when she felt a hand grab her ankle.

A voice below said, "Where do you think you're going?"

LAURA LOOKED DOWN AND saw Millie clinging to her leg.

"Millie, what are you doing?!" Laura said through gritted teeth.

"What are *you* doing?!" Millie whispered. "Get back down here before you get caught!"

"Let me go," Laura said, clutching the wall. "I'm going to find the Crystal Crown."

"The Crystal Crown? B-but how? And wh-where?" Millie sputtered.

Laura nodded toward the hills. "Out there."

"Out *there* is the worst *there* ever! You can't do this!"

"I'm going. There's nothing you can do to change my mind!" Laura flailed her leg, but Millie held on tight. It looked as if she were flying a kite in a hurricane.

"What if I begged?" said Millie.

"No."

"What if I cried?"

"No."

"What if I made you a gray pear pie?"

"That's literally the worst idea you've ever had."

Laura wrenched her leg away so strongly that Millie finally lost her grip. Laura pushed herself up on top of the wall, out of Millie's reach.

Millie stared up at her with big sad eyes. "Don't go."

"I'm sorry," said Laura. "But I have to. It's the only way to save Hillview."

Before Millie could protest any more, Laura dropped down onto the other side of the wall and landed in the soft dirt. Then she ran toward the hills, just like the orange fox. But she had barely made it a few steps when she heard a soft scream behind her, followed by a loud thud.

She turned around and saw Millie lying facedown in the dirt, her hair full of glowing green leaves. She had climbed up the tree and jumped. "Oof!" Millie groaned. "Really missed the landing on that one!"

Laura rushed over to her. "Are you okay?"

Millie sat up and clutched her knees to her chest. "I can't believe it! I'm outside the walls!" She trembled with terror. "You're outside the walls!"

"Yes, Millie, we're both outside the walls."

The color drained from Millie's face and she looked as though she was about to heave up a week's worth of rations. "Shouldn't we be dead by now?!"

Laura grabbed Millie's shoulders. "Why did you come after me? Have you lost your mind?"

"No, I haven't lost my mind! And I'm not going to lose my best friend, either. I'm not letting you do this alone."

Laura could hardly believe what she was hearing. She knew that Millie's fear of the outside world was a far bigger barrier than any stone wall. Yet, she was willing to fling herself into the unknown anyway.

Laura took Millie's shaking hands and pulled her to her feet. As always, Millie had a rucksack around her shoulder, the bottom sagging with gray pears.

"Are you sure you want to do this?" Laura asked.

Millie nodded.

"Okay, then. Let's go."

Together, they marched away from Hillview into the tree-covered landscape. Laura told Millie about her mother's notebook and about the last words she had written: *Bloato wears the Crystal Crown.* The sun rose higher in the sky. Millie wiped the sweat from her brow as they plodded up the nearest hill.

Just as they reached the top, they heard a chorus of voices echo through the valley: "Talamh'e." Earth.

They turned around and saw the walls of Hillview vanish under a cloak of Lysor magic.

***

After trekking through the hills for hours, Laura and Millie reached the top of a steep slope of dry dirt. Down at the bottom, they could see a cluster of houses made of dried black clay with wisps of smoke rising from the chimneys.

"Millie, look. A village!" said Laura with relief. She was beginning to worry that they might hike for days without seeing anyone.

Millie shifted her eyes nervously. "Do you think Bloato's down there?"

"Only one way to find out." Laura raced down the slope.

"Hey, wait up!" Millie called, running after her. She slipped on the gravelly bank and slid all the way down. She got up, rubbing the seat of her pants. "Talk about hitting rock bottom." She winced.

Laura helped her up, and they walked to the center of the village, where there was a crowded square. Vendors with carts full of goods stood at the edges. The townspeople looked just like Lysors, except none of them had locks of green hair.

Laura took a tunic out of her rucksack and tore off a strip of cloth. She tied it around her head like a bandanna so that it hid her glowing lock. Then she tore off another strip and handed it to Millie. "We should blend in."

"Good idea," Millie said, wrapping the cloth around her head. She breathed into her hand and sniffed. "I hope my breath doesn't smell too much like Thew."

"Don't worry, just try to relax."

"I'm calm! I'm relaxed!" Millie said in a strained voice that was neither calm nor relaxed.

They walked through an alleyway and entered the square. On a tall post was a wooden sign carved with the words THE DEAD END.

Millie shuddered. "Scary name for a town."

Laura grabbed her hand. "Come on."

They stopped at a cart where a woman was selling brightly colored clothing. There were silk shirts and velvet dresses, capes and trousers with elaborate patterns. Even though they had just left home, Laura already felt as if she were a thousand miles away from the bland beige tunics of Hillview.

"How do you make clothes with such brilliant colors?" Laura asked the woman behind the cart.

"Dye," she replied.

"Die?!" Millie shouted. "Laura, she's going to kill us!"

Laura elbowed Millie. "Wrong kind of 'dye,'" she said through gritted teeth. She feigned a laugh. "Sorry about her," she said to the woman. "She's got a weird sense of humor!"

She dragged Millie away, whispering, "Remember—calm and relaxed."

"Right! Sorry," Millie said.

They walked past a man selling hand-carved wooden instruments. There were rows of small flutes, drums with animal hides stretched over the tops, and guitars with big round bodies and long thin necks. The man picked up a guitar and strummed a chord. It was unlike anything Laura and Millie had ever heard.

They strolled by a wagon filled with colorful spices. The air was a swirl of exotic aromas. Millie took a big sniff and ended up sneezing an explosion of cinnamon.

That's when they saw something that stopped them both in their tracks. It was a cart piled high with fruits and vegetables. There was produce of all different shapes, sizes, and colors.

"Oh. My. Goodness," Millie whispered.

Laura's mouth started to water. "Let's go!"

They pushed their way through the crowd until they reached the produce cart.

Laura pointed to a bushel of bright orange carrots. "Look at those!"

"They're amazing!" Millie exclaimed.

The fruit seller, a stocky bald man wearing a dirt-stained smock, regarded them with amusement. "They're just carrots. Want to try?" He snapped a carrot in half and handed the pieces to Laura and Millie.

They bit into the carrots with a satisfying crunch. As they chewed, their faces lit up with wonder.

"That's the best thing I've ever had!" Laura marveled.

"We've got to find a carrot tree!" said Millie.

"Actually, we pull them out of the dirt," said the fruit seller.

"I don't even care." Millie beamed and took another bite.

"If you think that's good, try these!" the man said, handing Millie and Laura two ripe tomatoes. No one had ever been this enthusiastic about his produce before.

Laura took a bite out of the tomato. Bright red juice dribbled down her chin.

"It's bleeding!" Millie said with alarm.

"That's the juice," the fruit seller laughed.

"Juice," Millie repeated, intrigued. Gray pears had only chalky pulp.

The fruit seller saw something over Laura's shoulder, and the friendly smile on his face darkened. She turned to where the man was looking. There was a boy about her age wandering through the crowd, his eyes darting from side to side. He had rumpled blond hair and tattered clothes. He was so thin that Laura could see the outline of his rib cage through a hole in his shirt. She noticed something striking about him. One of his eyes was green, and the other one was violet.

"Watch out for that one," the fruit seller growled. "He's a thief."

Millie pulled her rucksack close to her chest.

As soon as the boy was gone, the fruit seller's smile returned. "Anything else you want to try? Help yourself."

Millie reached for a golden-brown onion, and before the

fruit seller could warn her, she took a gigantic bite. Her face turned red, and tears streamed down her cheeks.

"What is this?" she gasped.

"An onion," the fruit seller said. "Probably best not to eat it raw."

"Woo!" Millie said, wiping the tears from her bloodshot eyes. "I feel alive!"

Laura burst out laughing.

The fruit seller laughed, too. "You can keep that onion. It's on the house."

"Wow," Millie said, putting the onion in her rucksack. "Carrots from the dirt and onions from the house."

Laura put her arm around Millie. "See? The world isn't so scary after all."

Suddenly the square was filled with the sound of screaming as people fled in every direction. Laura turned and glimpsed the most terrifying creature she had ever seen in her life. It was the size of a large dog, with mangy fur and pointy ears. Its mouth was filled with sharp black fangs dripping oily drool. And it was running straight at her.

"LOOK OUT!" MILLIE SHOUTED, leaping on top of Laura and pulling her to the ground. The creature pounced and soared over Laura and Millie, its needle-sharp claws narrowly missing their heads. It came crashing down into the produce stand.

"Rotslobber!" the fruit seller screamed. He ran away as fast as he could, waving his arms in the air.

Laura and Millie scooted away in a panic, but they barely made it a few feet before their backs were up against a clay wall. They watched in horror as the rotslobber chomped into a ripe yellow grapefruit. As soon as its black fangs pierced the skin, the grapefruit instantly turned moldy and shriveled. The rotslobber devoured the putrid grapefruit with a disturbing snarl. Black drool rained down from its mouth, turning everything it touched rotten. Within moments, what had once been a bounty of fresh fruits and vegetables was now a graveyard of spoiled food, covered in flies. The rotslobber ravaged it with glee.

The town square was deserted now, except for Laura and Millie.

"Why did we ever leave Hillview?" Millie whimpered.

"We have to make a run for it," said Laura. She grabbed Millie's hand. "Now!"

They pushed themselves up, but as soon as they were on their feet, the rotslobber whipped its head around and let out a long, low growl.

"Good doggie," Millie squeaked.

It leaped down from the stand and stalked around them in a half circle.

At first Laura thought it was staring her right in the eyes, but then she realized it was actually staring at her hair. Laura touched her head. The bandanna was gone—it must have fallen off when Millie tackled her. The rotslobber's eyes fixated on her green lock. It bared its black fangs. And then charged.

Millie and Laura were too scared to even scream. The rotslobber was inches away from them when suddenly someone jumped onto its back, sending it off course.

It was the boy with the green and violet eyes.

The boy and the rotslobber hit the ground and rolled across the square. The beast snapped its jaws at the boy's neck, but he slipped out from under it just in time and sprang to his feet.

"Is that all you've got?" the boy shouted, trying to catch his breath.

The rotslobber licked its lips.

The boy backed away until he bumped up against the musical instrument cart. Without taking his eyes off the creature, he reached out and grabbed the neck of a wooden guitar. He held it above his head.

"Tier'e," he shouted.

The guitar burst into flames as if it had been lit with an invisible match.

Laura and Millie turned to each other and gasped.

The boy swung the flaming guitar at the rotslobber, but it was undeterred. It ran toward him. He swung the guitar again, this time connecting with the side of the creature's body. The smell of singed fur filled the air. The rotslobber let out a loud, angry howl that echoed through the square. Then it turned and ran away into the hills.

The boy dropped the guitar, and the crackling flames died down.

He ran over to Laura and Millie.

"Please don't hurt us!" said Millie, holding out her rucksack. "Take anything you want! It's mostly filled with gray pears."

The boy crouched down. He picked Laura's bandanna up from the ground and handed it to her.

Laura blinked in surprise. "Thank you."

Now that the rotslobber was gone, the townspeople were returning to the square. Laura noticed them giving her suspicious, unfriendly looks.

"You should get out of here," said the boy, his eyes flickering toward the crowd. "Follow me." He took off down a narrow alleyway.

Laura began to run after him. Millie grabbed her arm. "What are you doing? You trust him?"

"He saved our lives," said Laura. "And besides, he might know something about Bloato. I don't think anyone else is going to help us."

Millie eyed the townspeople, who were pointing at them and whispering. "Okay. Let's go."

Laura and Millie followed the boy through a labyrinth of alleyways until they reached a one-room clay house with boards over the windows and the door. The boy wiggled a board loose from the front window. He climbed inside the house and gestured for them to join him. Once they crawled inside, the boy replaced the board so that no one would be able to see in.

He reached out his hand, which was stained with black soot. "I'm Quin."

Laura and Millie introduced themselves.

The house was dark and drafty, the only light coming from the narrow slats in the boards. It was filled with strange objects—piles of old shoes, none of which seemed to match. Stacks of books with the pages folded as if Quin had read only part of each one. There was a coat that was definitely too big for him. And in the corner was a small straw bed covered by a threadbare blanket.

"Thank you for saving us from that—whatever that was," said Laura.

"Demon dog!" Millie cried.

"Rotslobber. From the Putrid Forest," said Quin.

"Where the Hexors live?" asked Millie.

Quin nodded. "The rotslobbers used to be trapped there just like the Hexors, but now they roam free."

"What happened?" asked Laura.

"Funny question coming from a Lysor. You're the ones who abandoned us."

"Abandoned you?"

"When you took the Crystal Crown all for yourselves and disappeared."

Laura was flabbergasted. "Is that what you think?"

He put his hands on his hips. "That's what everyone thinks. That's why I had to get you out of the square. Lysors aren't exactly welcome here."

Laura thought for a moment, taking this all in. "So why did you help us?"

"I think people should be judged for *who* they are, not *what* they are," said Quin, his green and violet eyes glowing in the dim light.

Laura took a step forward. "What are you?"

Quin dug through a pile of junk and pulled out a lumpy black candle. He set it on a table next to a wooden carving of an owl. "I'm a small mage. Lysors and Hexors have control over all of the elements. Regular people have control over—well, nothing. They can barely control their own tempers. Small mages, we're stuck in the middle. We can harness the power of a single element." He looked down at his hand. "In my case, tier'e." He flicked his thumb and forefinger, and a spark shot out, igniting the candlewick. The room brightened with yellow light.

"Fire," Millie whispered.

Laura knelt down in front of the candle and stared at the lumpy black wax. She'd never seen anything like it.

"That's a goblin wax candle," said Quin. "They're really rare."

"Where did you get it?" asked Laura.

Millie said under her breath, "He probably stole it."

"Millie!" Laura said through gritted teeth.

"It's okay," said Quin, his gaze dropping to the ground. "Everyone thinks that." He looked at Millie. "I bet you think I stole everything in here."

Millie didn't know what to say.

"If you want to know the truth, I didn't. Just because I couldn't pay for any of this doesn't mean I stole it. I collect what no one else wants, the stuff that gets left behind. Sometimes I keep it, sometimes I swap it. A while back, a trader passed through the market selling rare artifacts from all over the world. I gave him a gemstone I found in the hills, and in return, he gave me this goblin wax candle. It smells kind of weird, but it keeps the place nice and bright."

Millie took a step closer to him. "I shouldn't have said that. It's just, I've never been away from home and—well—things are different here, and—I'm sorry."

Quin's face softened. "Don't worry about it. I'm used to it. I've got to ask . . . Nobody's seen a Lysor in years, then you two show up in the Dead End to—what? Buy fruit?"

"We're looking for someone," said Laura.

"Oh, I can help with that!" said Quin with enthusiasm. "I've lived in the Dead End my whole life. I know everyone around here."

"Do you know someone named Bloato?" Laura asked.

Quin cocked his head. "No. I've never heard that name before."

But Laura pressed on. "Are you sure?"

"Positive," said Quin. "There's no Bloato here."

Laura felt a twinge of disappointment. She pushed herself to her feet. "If Bloato isn't here, we have to keep moving. We'll go to the next town." She extended her hand to Quin. "Thanks for helping us back there."

"Wait, wait, wait," said Quin. "The next town? We're in the middle of nowhere. That's why it's called the Dead End. It'll take days to get anywhere on foot. And the road is dangerous." He looked down at their flimsy sandals. "Plus, you don't exactly look like you spend a lot of time roughing it in the woods. No offense."

"What are we going to do?" Millie cried, throwing her hands in the air. "We already spent half the day getting here."

Laura paced back and forth. "What we need is a horse."

Quin's eyes lit up. "I can help get you a horse!" he blurted out. "I mean, not a horse *exactly*, but . . . well, you'll see."

Quin led Laura and Millie to the other side of the village, the area farthest away from the hills. They reached a long dirt road with a single house at the end. It was covered in such thick green ivy that the clay walls were barely visible. There was an expansive front yard full of giant shrubs carved into odd shapes.

They walked up the road, Quin in front and Laura just behind him. Millie was several paces back, looking around suspiciously. "Where are we?" she asked.

"Hobbly Knobbly's," said Quin.

Millie caught Laura's eye and mouthed, *"Who?"*

They reached the front yard. Laura looked closely at the carved bushes crowding the grounds. They looked like animals, but not animals Laura had ever seen before. One sort of resembled a bird, but it had hooves like a cow. Another could have been a snake except for its piglike snout. When a breeze blew by, the plant sculptures almost seemed to move.

Quin pressed his nose to one of the windows of the house. "Hello?" he called out. There was no answer. "Follow me," he said.

He led Laura and Millie behind the house to a big wooden barn with a pitched roof. Quin pushed the door open. It creaked loudly. A thick musty odor filled their nostrils. There was a row of stables with locked doors hiding the animals inside. Strange, unsettling noises came from behind the doors.

Quin grinned. "Wait till you see this. . . ."

But as soon as he took a step into the barn, a heavy burlap sack flew down over his head and shoulders, trapping him.

"Gotcha!"

A TALL MAN WITH LONG limbs and elbows like knotted wood grabbed Quin and dragged him deeper into the barn, the sack still over his head. The man's face was so worn, it looked like old leather.

"Trespasser!" he shouted in a raspy voice. He picked up Quin by the belt loops and tossed him into a trough full of filthy water.

Still outside, Laura and Millie ducked behind the barn door and watched through a hole in the wood, aghast.

Quin splashed around in the water, trying to get the sack off his head. "Help! Please!" he cried, his voice muffled by the burlap.

"Is it teatime?" Hobbly Knobbly bellowed. "Did I invite you in for a chocolate biscuit?" He pulled Quin up from the water.

"No!" Quin sputtered.

Hobbly Knobbly dropped Quin into the trough again.

"Is there a sign on my doorstep that says, 'Intruders welcome'?!"

Laura turned to Millie, who was biting her fist to keep from screaming.

"We have to do something," Laura whispered.

Millie nodded. "Like run away and never come back?"

"No, Millie!" Laura steeled herself and swung the barn door open. "Stop! It's not his fault! We're the trespassers!"

Hobbly Knobbly froze, holding Quin's head just above the water. He scowled at Laura and Millie. "Petty thieves!" He was about to dunk Quin again when Laura ripped the bandanna off her head.

"We're not petty thieves," she said. "We're Lysors."

"Lysors?" Hobbly Knobbly's mouth dropped open, and he let go of Quin, who splashed back into the water. As Hobbly Knobbly walked toward Laura and Millie, they saw his eyes—one green, one violet. He was a small mage, just like Quin. He gazed in awe at Laura's green shock of hair. "I don't believe it. Lysors! Incredible."

Quin climbed out of the trough and rolled onto the muddy ground. He ripped the bag off his head and gasped for air. "Why'd you have to do that, Hobbly?"

Hobbly Knobbly turned in surprise. "Oh, Quin! It's you. Why didn't you say something?"

"I would have, if you weren't stuffing me in the pig trough!" he said, wiping a glob of mud from his cheek.

"I don't have any pigs," said Hobbly. "That's just my bathtub."

"Gross!" Quin spat on the floor.

Hobbly tossed him a rag. "You should have known better than to sneak in here like that. I don't trust anyone these days." He turned back to Laura and Millie. "But Lysors—here in my barn! Amazing!" He brushed off his shirt and ran a hand through his wiry hair, trying to make himself presentable. "Where are my manners? Please, come in. Have a seat. Sorry about the smell in here."

Laura and Millie sat down uneasily on two short milking stools.

Hobbly Knobbly clapped his hands together. "Now. What can I do for you?"

"They need your help," said Quin, drying his hair with the rag.

"My help?" Hobbly chuckled. "Lysors need Hobbly's help. I never thought I'd see the day." His smile faded, and a realization flashed across his face. In a voice even softer than a whisper, he said, "The Lysors don't have the Crystal Crown, do they?"

Laura shook her head.

"I knew it!" he bellowed. He paced back and forth. "I knew the Lysors wouldn't leave with the Crystal Crown. I knew they wouldn't be so greedy. It's not the Lysor way!"

Millie and Laura shared a smile of relief. This Hobbly guy wasn't so bad after all.

"The Crystal Crown was stolen. That's why the Lysors went into hiding," Laura explained. "We thought the Hexors took it, but we were wrong."

"I could have told you that," said Hobbly. "Ever since the Hexors escaped the Putrid Forest, they've been searching for that crown, searching for the Lysors . . . There are rotslobbers everywhere, looking for a glimpse of green hair."

Millie's lip curled in disgust. "Hexors are horrible creatures."

Hobbly raised an eyebrow. "Funny, they say the same thing about the Lysors."

"Well, the Hexors found us," Laura explained. "They broke into our town, ransacked our homes, and said if we didn't hand over the crown, their entire army would destroy us."

Hobbly read her face like a book. "And you're out here looking for it."

Laura nodded. "I'm going to find the Crystal Crown and take it back to Hillview."

Quin shot to his feet. "You're going after the Crystal Crown? That is—"

Millie interrupted, "Insane? Ludicrous?"

"Awesome!" said Quin.

Millie sighed.

"We think someone named Bloato has it," said Laura.

Hobbly scratched his chin. "What kind of a name is Bloato?"

"What kind of a name is Hobbly Knobbly?" Quin muttered.

Hobbly pointed a long, crooked finger at Quin. "I'll have you know that I was named after my great-grandfather Hobilous Knobilous, and you'd do well to respect his great legacy!"

"What did he do?" Quin asked.

"He raced toads!" Hobbly said proudly. He turned back to Laura. "So who's this Bloato?"

"We don't know."

"Where does he live?"

"No idea," said Millie.

Hobbly arched his eyebrow. "Well, it sounds like you've got a well-thought-out plan."

Laura shot him a glare.

He tapped his fingertips together, deep in thought. "If you're looking for someone . . . Ah!" His eyes brightened as if a candle had just been lit inside his head. "You must visit Deirdre! She lives in the Marble City. Brilliant small mage. She may be able to help you. It'll be an arduous journey . . ."

"That's why we came here in the first place," said Laura. "We need a horse."

"Hmm, no horses here."

When he saw the look of disappointment on Laura's face, he assured her, "But I'm sure we can find you something!" He went over to the nearest stable and flung open the door.

There was a loud burp from the back of the stable, and

the air was filled with the smell of dead trout. Out came a small green dragon, waddling on two webbed feet, its wings hanging limply at its sides. It was no taller than Hobbly Knobbly's knees.

"Agh!" Millie jumped up, knocking over the stool. "What is that?!"

"It's okay, it won't hurt you," said Hobbly, looking slightly embarrassed. "This is a Draguin."

"A what?"

"A Draguin. It's a mix between a dragon and a penguin. That's what I do, I create new creatures right from the ground. I'm a small mage, like this one," he said, gesturing to Quin. "But I can't control fire. My element is earth. Talamh'e."

Laura thought about the strange bushes in the front yard. "So those shrubs and trees are . . . ?"

"Works in progress. I grow them, I sculpt them, then I bring them to life. But ever since the Lysors disappeared, my magic isn't what it used to be." He patted the Draguin on the head. "This little gal was supposed to be a mighty dragon-sized penguin that could soar through the sky and breathe fire.

Instead, I got a penguin-sized dragon that can't fly *or* breathe fire, but she does eat quite a lot of fish."

The creature burped again. Hobbly ushered it back into the stable and closed the door. He strode over to the next stable. "Let's see what we have here."

He opened the door, revealing a hideous creature with the head of a horse and a squat gray body with wrinkly skin and wiry hair springing out in odd directions.

Hobbly explained, "I was trying to make a Centaur—you know, half human, half horse. What I got was a Centaardvark. Half horse"—he let out a long sigh—"half aardvark."

Millie couldn't help but feel a little bad for the creature, whose body was almost buckling under the weight of its huge head. "Aw, it's kind of cute!"

Just then, the Centaardvark stuck its thin, straw-like tongue into the dirt and slurped up a mouthful of ants.

Hobbly shuddered. "It got the aardvark tongue, too." He shut the stable door. He strolled to the other end of the barn where there was a double-wide door. "Now this might be just the thing." He flung open the door. "A Cyclopopotomus!"

A huge one-eyed hippo bounded out into the barn.

"Hey, that could work!" said Quin.

Laura nodded in approval. It was definitely big enough to carry them.

Hobbly patted the Cyclopopotomus affectionately. "She's

strong, dependable. Even knows a trick! Watch!" Hobbly took an apple out of his pocket and threw it. "Fetch!"

The Cyclopopotomus charged after the apple. But then she ran right past it and crashed straight through the barn's back wall, sending bits of splintered wood everywhere.

Hobbly put his hands on his head, wincing. "I forgot. She has no depth perception. Well, that won't work." He put his hands to his mouth and called, "Come back, Karen!"

He turned to Laura and Millie. "Well, I guess that leaves us with only one option."

There was a nasally "Hee-haw!" from behind the last stable door.

Hobbly unlocked the latch. "It's a Donkeycorn. Part donkey, but with—"

"The magic of a unicorn?" Millie gasped, her eyes shining with excitement.

"No," Hobbly said, ashamed. "Just the horn of a unicorn."

The Donkeycorn clomped out of his stable. He was a short, big-eared donkey with a bristly mane that stood straight up and a small yellowish horn protruding from his forehead.

"So he doesn't fly or shoot rainbows out of his head?" Millie asked, disappointed.

Hobbly shrugged. "He doesn't do much of anything, unfortunately. Like all donkeys, he's a pretty good downhill climber." He tapped the end of Donkeycorn's twisted little horn. "And you could hang your coat on him, I guess."

Laura walked over to Donkeycorn. She looked at his round belly that sagged toward the ground, his goofy-looking smile full of big, square teeth. He wasn't exactly the mighty steed she'd had in mind, but he was big enough to carry her and Millie. And she knew Hobbly didn't have to give them anything at all. He could have thrown them out or, worse, thrown them in his bathtub.

Laura turned and extended her hand to Hobbly. "Thank you. We'll take good care of him."

Hobbly shook Laura's hand. "Be careful out there. It'll be a dangerous journey. It's good you'll have your Lysor magic to protect you."

Laura looked at the ground. "We don't know much about how to use Lysor magic. They don't teach us that anymore."

"We can make gray pears!" said Millie, reaching into her rucksack and handing one to Hobbly.

"Oh dear." Hobbly frowned. "It'll *really* be a dangerous journey. I'd go with you myself, but I'm a little too hobbly and far too knobbly."

Quin took a step forward. "I could go!" he said hopefully. "I know how to get to the Marble City. "I know which berries are safe to eat and which ones make your tongue fat and floppy. Plus, if you get cold, I could start a fire!"

Laura and Millie looked at each other, unsure.

"We *could* use someone who knows the land," said Laura.

Millie nodded. "That fire power could really come in handy. I did *not* bring enough layers."

"I promise I won't slow you down," said Quin.

"But what about your family?" Millie asked. "Won't your parents be worried?"

Quin and Hobbly locked eyes. "Parents?!" they said at the same time. They both nearly fell over laughing.

"No," Quin said, catching his breath. "It won't be a problem."

Laura and Millie gave each other a quizzical look.

"Well, I guess it's settled," said Laura. "I just hope we all fit on this Donkeycorn."

They led Donkeycorn to the front yard. Hobbly Knobbly loaded him up with as many jugs of water and extra blankets as he could carry.

"When you get to the Marble City, Deirdre's shop is the one with the eye on the door. She'll help you find this Bloato," he said. Then he handed Laura a leather-bound book with a green crescent moon on the cover. "An old Lysor friend gave this to me. Maybe it can teach you something about Lysor magic."

Laura smiled. "Thank you. For everything." She climbed onto Donkeycorn.

"I call middle!" said Millie, hopping up behind Laura.

Quin shrugged. "I guess that leaves me the rump." He climbed onto the back.

Donkeycorn took a step forward with a huff. It was a lot to carry.

They rode down the dirt road, waving good-bye to Hobbly.

He called after them, "I almost forgot! When you see Deirdre, tell her she owes me a fat goose!"

"Why?" Laura shouted.

"Years ago, I made a bet with her that the Lysors didn't abandon us." He put his hands on his hips and smiled. "And I was right!"

LAURA, MILLIE, AND QUIN rode for hours on the winding road that led away from the Dead End. The going was slow, and Donkeycorn was smelly. In fact, over the course of the afternoon, he'd managed to produce a variety of odors that led Millie to ask repeatedly what on earth Hobbly had been feeding him.

But it wasn't all bad. At one point, they rounded a bend and saw a field of brightly colored wildflowers. Laura was so stunned, she almost fell off Donkeycorn. Millie actually did fall off Donkeycorn. Even though they were in a hurry, they still took a few minutes to run through the field. After all, Laura thought, she and Millie might never have a chance to do it again.

As Laura ran, her hands outstretched so her fingers brushed thousands of soft petals, she remembered what her dad had said about wildflowers.

Like all the beauty of a sunset had sprouted from a tiny seed.

He was right.

Millie picked a handful of flowers and stuffed them in her face. "Ah, that's better," she said, inhaling deeply. "The inside of my nose was *all* Donkeycorn."

They continued riding until they reached a fork in the road.

"Okay," said Quin cheerily. "All we have to do is turn right here, and then we're on Easy Street."

"Really?" said Millie hopefully.

"Yup!" said Quin.

They rounded the bend and saw that the path led straight up a jagged granite mountain that rose up from the earth so high, it looked like it was piercing the sky.

"What?!" Millie cried.

Quin scratched his head. "I don't know why they named it Easy Street—it's actually really dangerous and difficult to navigate. But it's the only way to the Marble City!"

With no other choice, Laura steered Donkeycorn up the steep rocky path.

Quin was casually sitting backward behind Millie, snacking on some berries he'd picked along the way and flipping through the book Hobbly Knobbly had given to Laura.

"Wow!" he marveled. "Did you know that the Lysors once saved a town from a volcanic eruption?"

"Really?" said Millie.

"Yes! They reversed the flow of the lava just in time!

And check this out—" He pointed to the next page. "They once built a castle in the Frigid North made entirely of ice!"

"I hope they had extra blankets," said Millie.

A few moments later, Quin let out a loud "Whoa!"

"What is it?" Millie said, entranced.

"Have you ever heard of an Elemental Tornado? It combines earth, water, fire, and air into a single unyielding force."

"You're making that up," Laura scoffed.

"I'm reading it out of a book! Don't shoot the messenger." He read on, " 'In times when Lysor power was compromised, four Lysors could create an Elemental Tornado by summoning all the elements at once. It must be four Lysors—no more, no less.' "

"Well, I've never heard of that," said Laura. She was getting a little annoyed hearing about all the things the Lysors *used* to be able to do. It was no help to her now.

As they climbed higher and higher up the mountain, a chill rippled through the air. Millie huddled against Laura's back for warmth. Donkeycorn was getting slower and slower. Every time Laura tried to spur him on, he would just look back at her with that big dumb smile on his face. At one point, Quin even hopped off and tried to give Donkeycorn a little push. But Donkeycorn mistook Quin's push for a rump rub and slowed down to enjoy it even more. It seemed that no matter how hard they tried to get Donkeycorn to move at their pace, they were only going to move at Donkeycorn's pace.

Laura was worried. It was late in the afternoon already, and with each passing minute, their chance of finding the Crystal Crown and making it back to Hillview before the Hexors arrived was slipping away. She couldn't help but think that if there weren't two other people with her, not to mention all the supplies, Donkeycorn could have been able to move faster. But she didn't say it out loud.

As they neared the top of the mountain, the road stopped winding and got steeper and narrower. Soon, it was barely wide enough for Donkeycorn to put one hoof in front of the other. He had to walk in a straight line as though he were on an endless granite balance beam. Millie held on to Laura so tight that Laura found it hard to breathe.

"Millie, you're crushing my lungs!" Laura gasped.

"Sorry!" Millie squeaked, loosening her grip ever so slightly. "It's just that this is the scariest place I've ever been in my entire life."

"We'll be fine!" said Quin. "As long as Donkeycorn doesn't slip on any loose gravel."

"The whole road is loose gravel!" Millie cried.

"Hmm. Good point," said Quin.

Miraculously, they made it to the top without Donkeycorn slipping or Millie trembling so much that she toppled off on her own. When the road ended, they were faced with a sheer drop-off into a seemingly bottomless canyon. Because of the clouds hovering below them, it was impossible to

tell just how high up they were. A rickety rope bridge hung across the canyon.

Quin hopped off Donkeycorn. "Okay, all we have to do is cross this bridge, and then we'll reach the Marble City in no time."

"Let's go," said Laura. She hopped off Donkeycorn and stepped onto the first plank of the wooden bridge. Quin followed behind her. Millie brought up the rear, leading Donkeycorn. Even though he was on a wobbly bridge thousands of feet above the ground, he still had a big goofy grin on his face.

As they passed the middle of the bridge, Quin's foot landed with a *crunch*. He looked down. "Uh-oh. Peanut shells."

"What's wrong with peanut shells?" Millie asked anxiously. "Are you allergic? On your foot?"

"Peanuts are a troll's favorite food."

Laura's ears perked up. "Troll? You mean, like a troll that guards a bridge?"

"You mean, like a bridge that we're on right now?" Millie whimpered.

Quin scratched his head. "Uh-huh. There must be a troll nearby."

Laura and Millie looked frantically in every direction.

"There it is!" said Quin.

They spun around to look where Quin was pointing and saw an oddly shaped boulder at the far end of the bridge.

"Quin, I think you might need glasses," said Millie. "That's just a big lumpy rock."

"No, trolls turn to stone in sunlight! Looks like this one walked right into it," Quin laughed. "One thing about trolls, they've got a lot of hair but not a lot of brains."

Just then, they were hit with an icy chill. The sun had dipped below the mountain, casting long shadows across the canyon. In a matter of seconds, the darkness reached the far end of the bridge, covering the boulder.

The hard exterior of the rock cracked like an eggshell, and a hideous troll sprang to life.

LAURA, MILLIE, AND QUIN stopped in their tracks, staring in horror at the troll. It was twelve feet tall and covered in warts, with a big round belly that hung over the cloth wrapped around his waist.

Laura crouched down and whispered, "Stay still and be quiet."

"Okay," whispered Quin.

"Okay," whispered Millie.

"Hee-haw!" Donkeycorn screeched.

The troll grunted and turned, locking his bloodshot eyes on them. He pounded his fist on the bridge and let out an angry shout, revealing a single glistening tooth jutting from his pink gums.

There was only one thing to do.

"Run!" Quin shouted.

They ran back the way they had come, this time with

Donkeycorn in front. He clopped along the wooden planks as quickly as he could.

The troll climbed down under the ropes so he was hanging beneath the bridge. He swung from one wooden plank to the next like they were giant monkey bars. With his long limbs, he could swing much faster than Donkeycorn could run. He pulled himself back up onto the bridge, blocking their path. "Hot Breath angry!" the troll bellowed.

They stopped in their tracks.

"We're doomed!" Millie wailed.

Hot Breath shook the ropes with his big hands, and the bridge rattled violently. Everyone held on for dear life so they wouldn't get thrown into the abyss. Donkeycorn's motion sickness got the best of him, and he puked off the side of the bridge. The contents of his stomach were so gross that even Hot Breath grimaced.

Millie cringed in disgust. "What does Hobbly *feed* you?!"

Hot Breath jostled the ropes again.

Laura held on so tightly that her palms were rubbed raw. "Ow! Rope burn!"

Quin's eyes went wide. "That's it!" He snapped his fingers and called, "Tier'e!" igniting one of the hand ropes with a spark. The flames crackled toward Hot Breath, singeing the rope.

Laura grabbed Quin's wrist. "What are you doing?! You're going to burn the whole bridge down!"

Quin gasped. "Sorry! I should have thought that one through."

The flames reached Hot Breath's left hand. He let go of the rope, yelping in pain.

The fire got to the end of the rope and died out. With only one hand rope left, the bridge started to sag.

Hot Breath stuck his hand in his mouth, trying to cool the burn. Tears welled up in his eyes, and he shrieked at the top of his lungs, his high voice echoing off the canyon walls.

"He's going to kill us!" shouted Laura.

"Wait!" Millie took a step toward Hot Breath, her eyes narrowed. "I've seen this before!"

"You've seen a troll before?" Quin asked.

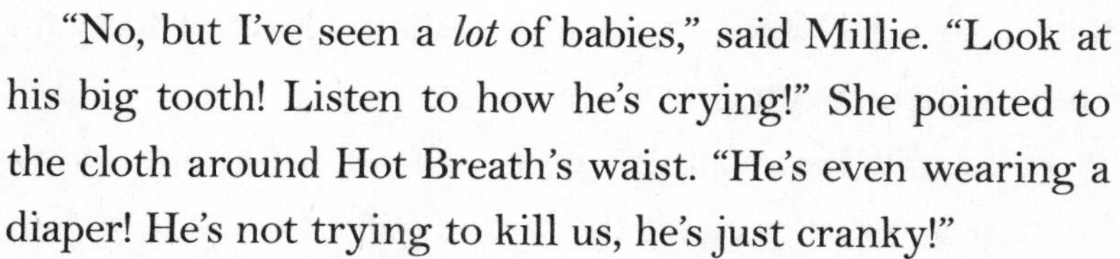

"No, but I've seen a *lot* of babies," said Millie. "Look at his big tooth! Listen to how he's crying!" She pointed to the cloth around Hot Breath's waist. "He's even wearing a diaper! He's not trying to kill us, he's just cranky!"

"Huh?" Laura and Quin said at the same time.

Millie inched her way toward the wailing baby troll. Big salty tears were dripping from his eyes. "There, there, Hot Breath. Millie's here," she said in the same soothing voice she used while comforting her baby brother, Georgie. She balled up her fist and gently pounded on his broad back.

Hot Breath let out a thunderous belch that blew Laura's and Quin's hair back.

"Whoa," said Laura. "I guess we know how he got his name."

"That's better, isn't it?" said Millie. "You're just a little gassy."

A look of relief passed over Hot Breath's face, and his eyelids started to droop.

"Millie," Laura whispered. "I think it's time for him to take a—"

"Don't say it," Millie warned.

"Nap."

Hot Breath's face twisted with rage, and he pounded his fists on the wooden planks. "No nap for Hot Breath!"

Millie held up her hands. "No nap, Hot Breath," she reassured him. "You can stay up as long as you want." She knew that very tired babies often needed to be tricked into falling asleep. "Rock the bridge!" she whispered to Quin and Laura through gritted teeth.

Quin and Laura pulled on the hand rope that wasn't burnt to a crisp, swaying the bridge gently.

Hot Breath lay down in a groggy stupor.

Millie sat down next to his big ear and stroked his matted hair. She began to sing Georgie's favorite lullaby.

Pick the fruit from the gray pear tree,
Forget all about your sorrows.
Take off the stem and spit out the seeds,
I'll cook you some Thew tomorrow.

The song was so soothing, even Donkeycorn's eyelids began to flutter. Hot Breath's eyes finally closed. Millie smiled at Laura and gave her a thumbs-up. They all tiptoed across the wobbly bridge as quietly as they could, leaving Hot Breath in a deep sleep, snoring softly—at least, for a troll.

By the time they reached the other side of the bridge, the sun had set completely.

"We'd better find some shelter for the night," said Quin.

They wandered a short distance off the road and set up camp underneath a big tree. Quin lit a fire to keep them warm, then went off in search of food for their dinner.

They were so high up in the mountains that in the light of the moons, they could see for miles in every direction. Even though she couldn't see her home, Laura could just make out the hills surrounding it. She pulled out the enchanted parchment paper and wrote to her dad just like she imagined her mother would have, without leaving a single detail out. The ink glowed green on the page, and Laura knew the enchantment was working.

Millie looked over Laura's shoulder in amazement. Laura

explained how the parchment worked, how her dad could be reading it right now. She included a message for her aunt Sage and uncle Simon, assuring them that Millie was okay. Actually, better than okay—she had saved the day.

"Dinner is ready!" Quin announced, shoving two steaming bowls of food under Laura's and Millie's noses.

"Thanks!" Laura said, taking one of the bowls.

Millie took the other. "How did you do that so fast?"

Quin shrugged. "If you know what you're doing, a forest is one big buffet. I hope you like it. All the ingredients are fresh and local!"

They slurped the bright green porridge from the bowls.

Millie scrunched up her face. "What's in it?"

Quin put his hands on his hips proudly. "Elderberry juice, stream water, some juniper seeds . . ."

"Why is it green?" asked Laura.

"Oh, that's the beetle butts."

Laura and Millie spat out the liquid onto the ground, startling Donkeycorn.

"Don't waste it!" Quin cried. "Beetle butts are an excellent source of protein."

Laura and Millie forced themselves to finish their dinner. Quin gobbled up his porridge hungrily and then made a bowl for Donkeycorn, who had no problem slurping up a bunch of beetle butts. Quin made the fire bigger, and they all warmed their hands around it.

"This was a fun day," he said.

"Fun?!" Millie exclaimed. "We almost plunged to our deaths at the hands of a hideous troll!"

Quin looked out toward the mountains. "I guess it's just nice to have company."

Laura puzzled over Quin. She had never met anyone like him. She thought about his one-room home filled with treasures others had left behind. It was clear he lived there by himself.

"Quin," she said. "When we asked about your parents earlier, what was so funny?"

"Oh that," Quin chuckled. "Small mages don't tend to have families. People think we're cursed. The moment my parents saw I had the eyes of a small mage, they took me as far as the road would go, dropped me in the Dead End, and left."

"That's horrible," said Millie.

"It's not all bad," said Quin. "It taught me to fend for myself. Plus, I get to stay up as late as I want." He let out a huge yawn. "Well, that's as late as I want."

He covered himself with a blanket and lay down.

"We should all get some rest," said Laura. "We'll leave for the Marble City at sunrise. We've got to find Deirdre soon."

Laura and Millie huddled together under a blanket, ready for sleep.

Quin looked up at the moons in the sky, his brow furrowed in thought. "Don't you think it's odd that the Lysors had the Crystal Crown for hundreds of years, and then suddenly someone was able to steal it?"

Laura and Millie looked at each other, perplexed. The thought had never occurred to either of them.

"It *is* odd," said Laura.

"How do you think that happened?" Quin asked.

A long moment of silence passed between the three of them, as no one could come up with an answer. Suddenly a strong gust of wind blew out the fire. They were all left in the dark in more ways than one.

THE MARBLE CITY WAS filled with more people than Laura and Millie had ever seen in their lives. The marble buildings gleamed white with swirls of blue and green. But despite the majesty of the ground level, the tops of the buildings looked like they had been demolished and hastily repaired. The roofs were made of a patchwork of driftwood and metal scraps. Horse-drawn carts barreled down the busy roads, and people rushed along the sidewalks past rows of storefronts—taverns, apothecaries, flower shops, and cobblers. They all wore sturdy, broad-brimmed hats. Several people who passed Laura and Millie looked suspiciously at their bandannas. But Laura and Millie were too busy marveling at the city to notice. They stood, awestruck, until one of the horse-drawn cart drivers hollered, "Get out of the way!"

They pulled Donkeycorn out of the road, just narrowly avoiding a collision.

"This place is wild," said Millie.

"What happened to the roofs?" Laura asked.

"From what I hear, after the Lysors disappeared, the Marble City developed"—Quin hesitated, trying to find the right words—"a bit of a bird problem." He pointed to a storefront down the street that had a red door with a large eye carved into it. "There it is! The shop with the eye on the door!"

They tied up Donkeycorn outside and pushed open the door. A copper bell rang as they walked in. They found themselves in what appeared to be a drab waiting room filled with people crowded on wooden benches. Some sat patiently, while others twiddled their thumbs anxiously, looking back and forth.

Sitting behind a desk was an old woman with white, wispy hair tied up in a bun so it looked like there was a big cotton ball growing on the top of her head. Her eyes were glued to a book. She didn't even glance up as Laura approached her.

Laura cleared her throat. "We're looking for Deirdre?"

"Take a number," the woman said in a monotone voice, pushing a stack of parchment toward Laura. The piece on the top said *23*. Laura looked around nervously at the crowded room. They didn't have time to wait for all these people to see Deirdre.

"Please," Laura tried. "It's important."

The woman raised her eyes from her book, meeting Laura's. "Kid, everyone walks in here acting like if they don't see Deirdre right away, the whole world is going to end. Here's the truth—it's not!"

Laura dropped her voice to a whisper. "But Hobbly Knobbly sent us."

"I don't care who sent you, Hobbly Knobbly or Hubbly Wubbly or Hoobly Scoobly! Everyone has to take a number!" she snapped.

By now, the whole room was staring daggers at Laura. She sheepishly took the number and squeezed onto a bench in between Millie and Quin.

They overheard a conversation on the bench next to them.

"So why are you here?" said a woman with wire-rimmed glasses.

A man in dirty overalls replied, "Someone stole my cow. I've got to get it back. I haven't had milk for days. What about you?"

"I'm in a book club, and I have a sneaking suspicion that *I'm* the only one who reads the books!"

Laura, Millie, and Quin exchanged confused glances.

Millie whispered, "What do you think this Deirdre lady actually does?"

Laura and Quin shrugged.

Just then, the door at the back of the room flew open. An old man with a curved back and a wooden cane walked out, followed by a tall woman with long, straight black hair and silver bracelets stacked on her wrists. She had the eyes of a small mage, one green eye and one violet.

The man shook her hand enthusiastically. "Thank you, Deirdre, I've always wanted to know what my cat does while I'm at work."

"You're very welcome," Deirdre said, waving good-bye. As soon as the man walked out, Deirdre turned to the woman behind the desk and shrugged. "It's not that interesting. The cat just sleeps all day."

"Number seven!" the woman behind the desk called out.

The man in the dirty overalls stood up. Laura knew she had to do something. There was no time to spare. She ran over to Deirdre.

"Excuse me, Deirdre?" she said. She pulled back her bandanna ever so slightly, just enough to reveal her green lock to Deirdre alone.

Deirdre drew in a sharp breath. "I owe Hobbly Knobbly a fat goose, don't I?"

Laura nodded.

Deirdre clapped her hands and announced, "Everybody out, we're closed for the day."

"But my cow!" the man in the overalls whined.

"Come back tomorrow," said Deirdre. "Martha, you can go, too."

The woman behind the desk shut her book and stood up. "Okay, but I expect to be paid for a *full day*."

Everyone filed out of the room, grumbling and complaining. Martha left last, locking the door behind her.

Deirdre looked to Laura, then Millie, and finally locked eyes with Quin. "This day just got a lot more interesting." She smiled. "Come with me."

They followed Deirdre into the back room. Everything was made of marble—the walls, the floor, and a large basin in the center of the room that was filled with water. There were blue velvet stools positioned around the basin. A large window on the back wall looked out onto a beautiful tree-filled courtyard.

"Wow." Quin arched his eyebrow. "Being a small mage in the big city is pretty different."

"Nobody trusts a small mage until you help them find their lost cow. Then suddenly you're their best friend." Deirdre winked at Quin, then sat down on the stool closest to the window. "It's been a long time since I've seen a Lysor. You must have traveled quite a ways."

"We have," said Laura. "All the way from the Dead End."

"How's Hot Breath doing?" Deirdre asked.

"Cranky," Millie replied.

"Well, he's still teething. Trolls live to be seven hundred years old. It takes them a while to mature. Now, something tells me you didn't come here to chitchat." She gestured for them to sit down. "Whose eyes?"

"Sorry?" Laura asked.

"Whose eyes would you like to see through? That's what I do. Anyone you want, I can show you what they're seeing at this very moment."

"Really?" Millie asked. "Is my little brother Horton reading my diary?"

"If he's your little brother, then yes," said Deirdre. "I don't need any magic to tell you that."

Laura piped up, "Bloato. We need to see through the eyes of Bloato."

"Bloato it is," Deirdre said. She leaned over the stone basin. Her chin hovered just above the water. She glanced up at Laura. "What are you waiting for? Make me cry."

"What?" said Laura.

Deirdre sighed. "Martha didn't tell you? I need you to make me cry. That's how this works. My tears fall into the water basin. We see through this Bloato person's eyes. Couldn't be simpler," Deirdre said matter-of-factly. "But don't try any sob stories, I already heard one today that you'll never top. It was about a guy who accidentally ate his pet fish. So sad when that happens!"

Millie thought for a moment. "Sometimes I laugh so hard, I cry. I know! I'll tell you a classic Lysor joke." She rubbed her hands together. "Okay. Why did the Never-Dark Forest trees blow away in the wind? Because they were so *light*!" Millie burst out into hysterical laughter. "Get it?!" she shrieked, doubling over.

Deirdre stared at her blankly.

"Millie," Laura said. "Deirdre doesn't know what the Never-Dark Forest is. Plus, it's not a very good joke."

Millie wiped away tears from her own eyes. "Agree to disagree, Laura," she said, still giggling. "Agree to disagree."

"I know!" Quin said, waggling his fingers. "Are you ticklish?"

Deirdre held up her hand. "Don't even think about it!"

Laura racked her brain. There had to be some way to make this woman cry. They couldn't have come all this way for nothing. Suddenly her eyes went wide. "I've got it!" She grabbed Millie's rucksack and pulled out the big brown onion she had gotten from the produce cart in the Dead End.

"Genius!" said Quin.

"Keep that thing away from me," said Millie.

Laura peeled off the outer layer of the onion, then snapped it in half and held it under Deirdre's nose. Deirdre took a deep breath in. Tears welled in her eyes.

"Ooh!" she said. "Here come the waterworks."

The tears rolled down her cheeks and into the basin with a soft *plunk!* At that exact moment, Deirdre said, "Oighar'e."

Water.

Dark blue droplets swirled on the surface of the basin as if it were filling with ink.

When the droplets cleared, an image appeared, fuzzy at first, like the memory of a dream. Then it came into focus. It was a dark room with walls made of rock. It was filled with jewels and precious metals, shiny gold coins piled high in the corners. Whoever this Bloato was, they couldn't see him, but they could see through his eyes that he was seated on a golden throne. He brought a silver chalice to his lips and took a long sip. Then he stood and crossed the opulent room, his silk robe dragging along the stone floor. The room was dimly lit with lumpy black candles.

Laura recognized it instantly. It was the same kind of candle that Quin had lit in his tiny house. "Quin, those are—"

"Goblin wax candles," he finished her thought.

They looked back into the basin.

Bloato stood in front of a long table where there was a ruby-encrusted box. He reached out his hands, which were a sickly green. His nails were long and yellow. His fingers were covered in heavy gold rings with fat diamonds. He opened the box. When Laura saw what was inside it, she teared up a little herself.

It was a crown carved entirely of crystal so clear, she could see right through it.

As Laura stared at the image of the Crystal Crown in the pool of water, her lock of hair became so bright that it cast a green light throughout the whole room. Heat radiated through her entire body. Then suddenly a bright light came in through the window. The trees in the courtyard outside were glowing more brightly than the Never-Dark Forest.

All at once, the image in the basin disappeared. The water became clear, and Laura found herself staring at her own reflection. Her lock dimmed, and the trees outside stopped glowing.

Quin stared at Laura. "What. Just. Happened?"

Deirdre looked at Laura. "You found what you were looking for."

"I can't believe it!" Millie said. "We actually saw it!"

Quin jumped to his feet. "We've got to go get it."

Millie and Quin headed for the door, but Laura didn't move. She didn't speak. She just kept thinking of the words her mother had written, *Bloato wears the Crystal Crown.* All those years ago, she had been right.

"Laura, come on!" Millie said.

Laura looked back up at Deirdre. She knew she would never have a chance like this again. "I need to see through one more person's eyes."

Deirdre placed her hands on the sides of the basin. "Whose?"

Laura took a deep breath. "My mom's."

The look of longing on Laura's face brought a tear to Deirdre's eye without the help of any onion. It dropped into the basin.

"Oighar'e," Deirdre said.

Laura watched the blue droplets dance across the surface of the water. Her heart raced. For a moment, she felt the faintest glimmer of hope. But then, when the droplets cleared, there was only darkness.

Deirdre placed her hand on Laura's. "I'm sorry."

From outside, they heard the sound of giant wings flapping overhead.

Deirdre looked up, panic flashing across her eyes. "Scabenger!"

Before Laura could take a single step, an enormous black beak pierced through the ceiling and tore off the roof.

LAURA DUCKED FOR COVER as the vulture-like scabenger spat out the chunk of roof. Its wingspan stretched longer than the entire room. Its face was so red, it looked like it had a terrible sunburn. Its eyes were the size of fists. Black drool dribbled from its hooked beak and splattered onto the onion on the floor. When the drool hit the onion, it shriveled and rotted instantly.

The scabenger pecked its gigantic beak downward, and Laura rolled away just in time.

"I told you they had a bird problem," Quin called from the corner.

"That's the understatement of the year!" said Millie, covering her head with her arms.

"It must have seen the trees glowing," said Deirdre, her back pressed against the wall. "It knows there are Lysors here!"

Laura ran to the door and was about to fling it open

when the scabenger swooped down into the room, its wrinkly legs looking like burnt tree branches. It opened its mouth and let out a screech that sounded like a thousand nails scraping glass. It thrust its head at Laura and opened its beak. Just as it was about to chomp down, Deirdre shouted, "Oighar'e!"

With a flick of her wrist, the water in the basin rose up in a wave and flew across the room, splattering into the scabenger's eyes. The scabenger recoiled just long enough for Laura to open the door.

"Let's go!" she commanded. She ran into the front room with Millie, Quin and Deirdre following. She leaped over the wooden benches and unlocked the front door, then ran out onto the street. She could hear the scabenger screeching in rage, unable to fit through the back doorway.

As soon as they were all outside, Deirdre slammed the front door behind her. "You have to get out of the city. It'll stop at nothing!"

Quin untied Donkeycorn, who, despite the chaos, was still grinning like it was the best day of his life. Quin helped Millie up.

Deirdre pointed ahead. "The goblins live that way, beyond the cliffs. Go!"

Laura turned to her. "Where will you go?"

"I'll be fine here," said Deirdre. "It's not after me."

Laura was about to go when Deirdre grabbed her wrist. "Wait." She stared at Laura intensely with her green and violet eyes. "I saw the strength of your power in there, Laura. Don't be afraid to use it."

Laura was taken aback.

"Come on!" Quin called.

Laura nodded at Deirdre. "Thank you."

She rushed over to Donkeycorn and gave him a slap on the rear. Startled, Donkeycorn sped off. It was the fastest he had ever run. Laura sprinted alongside him until she was able to grab on to his horn. In a single swift movement, she pulled herself onto his back without slowing him down.

At that moment, the scabenger soared through the giant hole it had ripped in Deirdre's roof and into the sky. It flapped its gigantic wings and let out an ear-piercing screech. The entire city plunged into a panic. Some people rushed into the nearest storefronts, others crouched behind the tall buildings. Others just held on tightly to their broad-brimmed hats and hoped for the best. The cart drivers veered their horses off the road to try to find cover.

Donkeycorn's hooves clip-clopped against the marble ground. As they passed a tipped-over pastry cart, he slowed down to take a bite out of a loaf of bread.

"No, Donkeycorn!" Laura, Millie, and Quin shouted all at

once. They kicked at his side and yelled words of encouragement, but only after he'd gobbled up the entire loaf did he pick up speed again.

As they dashed through the city, the sound of wings flapping overhead seemed to multiply. Laura saw that two more scabengers were flying alongside the first one.

"Millie," Laura called back. "Whatever you do, don't look up."

"Huh?" Millie said, immediately looking up. *"Aaagh!"*

Laura pulled Donkeycorn to the right, and they turned down a narrow street with tall buildings on either side. One of the scabengers spotted them and swooped down behind them, its flapping wings shattering the second-story windows. It knocked its wing against the marble siding of a building and crashed to the ground.

Donkeycorn was galloping faster than ever now. They followed the road all the way to the outskirts of the city, where there were no more tall buildings to give them cover. The two remaining scabengers converged in the air behind them, screeching menacingly.

"They're gaining on us!" said Quin.

Laura kept her eyes straight ahead. What she saw filled her with almost as much terror as the giant birds. Nothingness. They were heading straight toward the edge of a cliff.

"Whoa!" she shouted as Donkeycorn slid to a stop so close that he sent rocks flying over the edge. "Millie, whatever you do, don't look down," she said.

Millie immediately looked down. *"Aaagh!"*

The scabengers dipped low to the ground, zooming toward them. They were moments away from being torn apart by two razor-sharp beaks. Then Donkeycorn did something utterly shocking. He leaped off the edge of the cliff.

Laura felt her stomach do a somersault as they plunged downward. But then Donkeycorn's hooves landed on a rock jutting out of the cliff.

Millie's hands were covering her eyes. "Are we dead?" she whimpered.

But they weren't. Far from it. Donkeycorn expertly lurched from one protruding rock to the next. Hobbly Knobbly was right—Donkeycorn was an expert downhill climber. Laura and Millie clung to Donkeycorn's mane, and Quin held desperately to his tail to keep from teetering off.

The scabengers flew out over the cliffside and trained their eyes on Laura. As they nose-dived, Donkeycorn squeezed between two tall boulders into an opening so narrow, he could barely fit his big belly in. Laura, Millie, and Quin scrambled off Donkeycorn and crouched down, hiding themselves from the scabengers' view. The scabenger beaks hit the tops of the boulders, chipping off shards of rock, but the opening was too narrow for them to fly inside. After a long while, the pecking finally stopped. The scabengers gave up and flew away, their angry shrieks fading into the distance.

Laura threw her arms around Donkeycorn's neck and nuzzled his cheek. "You did it, Donkeycorn!"

Quin patted Donkeycorn heartily on the back. "Donkeycorn saves the day!"

"He may not have any unicorn powers, but he sure has donkey powers!" said Millie.

Donkeycorn brayed, his smile growing even wider than usual. They all climbed back on, and he carried them all the way down to the bottom of the cliff. There they found a rushing river, and Donkeycorn bowed his head to take a drink. Quin splashed water on his face.

Laura looked around. "Now that we know Bloato is a goblin, how are we going to find him?" She felt like she was so close to the crown. She had even seen it with her own eyes—or, rather, with Bloato's eyes. But now she didn't know which way to go.

Up the river, a fisherman was standing knee-deep in the water, casting his line. There wasn't anyone else for miles. He might be the only one who could help them.

Laura approached him, and Millie and Quin followed.

"Excuse me," Laura called from the riverbank. "Do you live around here?"

"Not far," said the fisherman.

"This may sound strange, but . . . are there any goblins around here?"

"Ugh! Goblins!" The fisherman spun around, half tangling himself in his fishing line. "I wish there weren't. This area is teeming with them. Horrible creatures. Never trust a goblin."

"Do you know where we could find them?" Laura asked.

"I've heard they live in a cave. It's not far. But you don't want to go there. They don't take kindly to outsiders."

"I'm afraid we're going to have to risk it."

The man furrowed his brow. "Well, there are two ways to get there." He pointed up ahead where the river split in two directions. "You can go east toward Bog Belly, but that's a terrible idea! It's a stinking, festering pit full of horrible mud goons that'll chomp you up like chicken wings!"

Millie raised her hand. "I vote no on going that way!"

"What's the other way?" Laura asked.

"You can go south, but that's a horrible idea!"

"Why?"

"It goes right through the Putrid Forest! It's full of Hexors and rotslobbers and scabengers that'll chomp you up like chicken wings!"

Quin threw his hands in the air. "So either way, we're going to get chomped up like chicken wings?"

"I'm afraid so," said the fisherman.

Laura weighed the two options. She knew that their best chance of survival was to stay as far away from the Hexors as possible. The choice was clear. "We're going to Bog Belly."

"If you say so," said the fisherman, holding up his hands. "But don't say I didn't warn you."

Laura began walking down the rocky bank toward the fork in the river. Millie and Quin eyed each other warily but followed behind with Donkeycorn.

The fisherman called after them, "Why do you want to go looking for goblins anyway?"

Laura turned to him. "They took something that belongs to us. I'm going to get it back."

BOG BELLY WAS A vast pit of murky brown mud. Bubbles formed on the oily surface. When they popped, they released a smell like rotten eggs. Bare trees with thin strands of algae hanging from the branches rose from the mud like zombies.

Donkeycorn stood at the edge of the bog with Laura, Millie, and Quin on his back.

Laura grimaced. "This thing looks like the world's biggest bowl of Thew."

"Excuse me!" huffed Millie.

Far on the other side of the bog, they could see a craggy rock formation in the distance. Laura pointed ahead. "There. All we've got to do is make it across this stink pot, and we'll be at the goblin cave."

"I just hope somebody doesn't mistake us for a chicken wing first," said Millie.

"A little mud never hurt anybody," said Quin. "Plus, it can't be as bad as Hobbly Knobbly's bathtub."

Donkeycorn stepped into the mud with a sickening *squelch.* As always, he had a big goofy grin on his face, but his eyes were full of dread. As Donkeycorn waded through the bog, Laura searched the surface for any sign of movement. Quin stuck two berries in his nostrils to use as nose plugs. Millie was so nervous, she squealed every time one of the big bubbles popped.

"Shh!" said Laura. "Stay quiet!"

"Sorry," Millie whispered. That's when she noticed Laura's lock of hair. The farther they moved across the bog, the brighter it glowed, even under her bandanna. "Laura, your hair!"

Laura turned around and saw that Millie's lock was glowing brighter, too. She smiled. "We're getting close to the Crystal Crown."

The mud was almost up to Donkeycorn's knees now, and it was getting thicker. Donkeycorn had to pry his hooves up with all his strength just to move through the goop. Each step was more difficult than the last.

Laura saw another bubble rise up from the muck, the biggest one yet. But it didn't pop like the others. That's when she realized it wasn't a bubble at all. It was a perfectly round, bald head.

"Mud goon!" Laura shouted.

The mud goon sprang up from the bog. It was tall,

slender, and practically faceless—no eyes, no nose, just a gaping hole for a mouth. It was dripping from head to toe with thick mud. It skittered across the surface so fast that Donkeycorn didn't even have time to turn around. Then, without making a sound, the mud goon wrapped its long fingers around Millie's ankle. It pulled her down under the slimy mud. The whole thing happened in seconds.

"Millie!" Laura screamed.

Donkeycorn reared up in terror.

Without a second thought, Laura dove into the mud and started frantically searching for Millie.

Donkeycorn bolted in a panic, carrying Quin with him. "Donkeycorn, no!" Quin cried, trying to stop him. He splashed through the mud in a frantic circle, letting out high-pitched brays but still smiling like a buffoon.

Laura finally felt Millie's arm underneath the wet, slippery muck. She grabbed on and yanked as hard as she could, pulling Millie up.

Millie gasped for air, her head coated in mud. "Help!" she cried, coughing up algae.

Laura pulled Millie in close. The mud goon emerged behind her. It grabbed on to Millie's other arm, but Laura held on tight. Laura and the mud goon faced off in a flailing game of tug-of-war—and Millie was the rope.

Meanwhile, on the other side of the bog, Quin was trying to get control of Donkeycorn.

"Easy, boy. Easy," he said, trying to sound soothing.

But the harder Quin tried, the more Donkeycorn stumbled around in the slippery filth.

Then more bald heads appeared. It was like a mud rooster had crowed and all the mud goons were waking up for breakfast.

Five of them rose up, surrounding Quin and Donkeycorn.

Fortunately, Quin was able to snap a dry branch off a nearby tree and set it on fire. Unfortunately, as soon as he swung it at one of the mud goons, it wrapped its wet fingers around the flame and extinguished it immediately.

"I take it back!" Quin said, his voice trembling. "I'd rather be in Hobbly Knobbly's bathtub!"

Laura was losing her grip on Millie's arm.

"Don't let go!" Millie screamed.

Laura knew Millie could slip from her grasp at any moment, and then she would be lost forever. The mud goon wrenched Millie away, causing Laura to fall face-first. She

pulled herself up, but her bandanna was still stuck in the bog. As Laura shook the mud off, she spotted a glimpse of her green lock glowing more brightly than it ever had in her life. She remembered what Deirdre had said—*I saw the strength of your power in there, Laura. Don't be afraid to use it.* Across the bog, the mud goons were crawling up Donkeycorn's legs. Quin kicked at them frantically, screaming something about how he didn't want to die in a soup of stinky mud.

Laura saw the mud goon wrap its fingers around Millie's shoulders, about to bring her down. She lunged forward and grabbed Millie's hands, then shouted, "Talamh'e! Oighar'e!"

After all, she thought, *what more was a mud goon than earth and water?*

She could feel Lysor magic coursing through her body as her lock burned bright. The mud goon let out a shriek of pain as it split into a puddle of clear water and a cloud of dry dirt, its very essence torn in half.

The other mud goons immediately stopped in their tracks, terrified by what had just happened. They let go of Donkeycorn's horn and Quin's scrawny legs and splashed down into the mud, disappearing below the frothy surface.

Donkeycorn galumphed over to Laura and Millie. He was so coated in mud, he looked a bit like a goon himself.

Quin reached out his arm and pulled up Laura and then Millie. "Laura, what *was* that?!"

Millie was shaking all over, still in shock. "I—I was going to ask the same thing. Where did you learn to do that?"

Laura tried to come up with an explanation, but she had no words for it. It was like asking a bird how it had learned to fly. "I don't know," Laura said to Millie. "I just knew I had to save you."

"Well, thank Lysoria you did!" Millie cried. "You don't even want to know what it was like down there. It was like being trapped in a rotten egg. A rotten *fish* egg . . . full of barf!"

"It's okay, Millie," said Laura.

"Okay?! I almost died!"

"Well, you're safe now," Laura said, trying to comfort her. "Just try to forget about it."

"I'll never forget about it," said Millie. "I could spend the next ten years swimming in the Clear Lake, and I still won't get this stench off me."

As they crossed the bog, Laura was exhausted. She felt like she had been awake for days. She thought about how weak her dad had become after he'd driven out the Hexors. What if she needed to use Lysor magic again? What if she couldn't? Her head hurt. And all the while, Millie was talking nonstop about falling into the bog.

By the time they made it to the other side, they had never been so happy to get their feet on dry land. The goblin cave was just a short distance ahead. The entrance loomed like a dark moonless night.

Millie shuddered. "I just hope it's not as dark in there as it was under the mud. Seriously, you have no idea how dark it was down there! It was like when you close your eyes, but times ten thous—"

"Millie!" Laura snapped. "We don't know what's waiting for us in the cave, and if you're going to be so scared all the time, maybe you should just wait out here."

Millie winced as if Laura had just thrown a glass of cold water in her face. "You don't want me to come with you?" she said meekly.

Laura could see that she'd said the wrong thing. "Well, I don't know! I just—"

"But I came all this way."

"Okay. I didn't mean it." Laura sighed. "Let's go."

Laura stomped ahead, and Millie followed. Quin lagged a little behind with Donkeycorn, wanting to stay as far away from the tension as possible.

As they got closer to the goblin cave, they saw that it was being guarded by a goblin carrying a long, sharp spear.

They ducked behind a tree.

"How are we going to get past that guard?" said Quin. "And more importantly, what happens when we get inside the cave? We can't exactly blend in, especially you two. Your hair is glowing like fireflies!"

"There's got to be a way," said Millie, trying to sound brave.

"There *is* a way," said Laura. She pulled the bottle of Chamelixir from her pocket and showed it to them. "It's an ancient Lysor tonic."

"Your dad gave you that?" Millie said, astonished.

Laura nodded. "It's called Chamelixir. It helps you blend into any surrounding."

"How?"

Laura paused. "I'm not exactly sure. All I know is that once we take it, we can't use any magic or it will reverse the effects." She pointed at Quin. "So no fire."

Quin held up his hands. "Hey, you're the one who just ripped a mud goon in half."

"Here goes nothing," Laura said, unscrewing the top of the tiny glass bottle. She didn't know how much was left, she just hoped it was enough for all of them. One by one, they each took a small sip.

There was a creaking sound like an old door opening as their ears began to stretch and their backs hunched over. Their feet got bigger until the straps of their leather sandals burst and their skin faded into a sickly green. The ends of their teeth became prickly. Their noses were filled with the horrid smell of their own breath, like stale meat. Their stomachs bloated into big round potbellies, and all at once their belly buttons turned from innies to outies with a *pop!*

"We're all hideous goblins!" Millie cried.

Quin looked at his hands and rubbed his belly. "I think I'm a pretty good-looking goblin."

"Hee-haw!" Donkeycorn brayed.

"What are we going to do about him?" said Millie. "We can't just leave him here."

"You're right," said Laura. "But he'll attract way too much attention in there." She looked down at the bottle. It was worth a try. "Bottoms up, Donkeycorn!" she said, pouring the last drops onto his tongue.

The Chamelixir worked just as well on Donkeycorn as it had on Laura, Millie, and Quin. He shrunk down to the size of a goblin, his hooves transformed into big ugly feet, and his ears—well, his ears stayed pretty much the same shape and size, but now they were green.

Laura nodded, satisfied. "You'll blend in perfectly!"

"Hee-haw!" said Donkeycorn with the same goofy smile as always, though now it was filled with sharp goblin teeth.

"As long as you stay quiet," Laura added. She grabbed Donkeycorn's hand and helped him walk on two feet for the first time in his life. The four goblins headed to the entrance of the cave.

LAURA, MILLIE, QUIN, AND Donkeycorn had no problem getting past the goblin guard. After all, they looked as green and gross as he did. As they approached him, he rubbed his big belly like it was some sort of greeting. So Laura did the same back. He stepped out of the way and let them in. At the entrance was a narrow tunnel. As they walked deeper inside, they heard strange noises up ahead.

"What do you think they're doing in there?" Millie whispered.

"I don't know," Quin said. "But it's not going to be pretty. Goblins are malicious and devious. They're probably grinding up bones or fighting over the few scraps of food they can get their grubby hands on."

They turned a corner, and the tunnel opened up, revealing a cavern nearly as big as Hillview. Their mouths dropped.

"Are they having a *party*?" said Laura.

Massive stalactites hung from the ceiling, draped in elaborate crystal chandeliers with black goblin wax candles that filled the vast cavern with flickering light. Gold and rare gemstones were piled high in every corner of the cave. And the place was packed with goblins who appeared to be having the time of their lives. The strange sound was actually goblin music—a lively band was playing on a big flat rock that served as a stage. It was the most horrible music Laura had ever heard—accordions yowling like hungry cats, bagpipes bleating like angry goats, and the *tap-tap-tap* of a single goblin thwacking a wooden spoon on his bony knee. But the crowd seemed to be loving it. There was a throng of goblins dancing gleefully at the foot of the stage.

"Well, I guess I was wrong about what goblins do," said Quin.

"Let's find Bloato, get the crown, and get out of here," said Laura. "I don't know how much music my ears can take."

They made their way through the crowded cave, Laura leading Donkeycorn by his goblin hand. They walked past a pile of gold coins so high, it almost reached the ceiling. Two goblins slid down it like it was a snowy hill, squealing in delight. They stepped over a drooling goblin who was taking a nap on the floor, his head resting on a diamond-encrusted pillow and his body covered in a blanket of silver chains.

Some rowdy goblins were playing a game that involved throwing a ruby the size of a fist into a big silver chalice. A goblin wearing a leather vest landed the ruby in the chalice, and the whole gang cheered.

"That's a new record!" one goblin said, slapping the leather-vested goblin on the back. "Way to go, Tortle!"

The goblin named Tortle grinned. "Who thinks they can beat me?" He looked around and pointed straight at Millie. "You there!"

"Me?" Millie said, trying not to sound terrified but definitely sounding terrified.

"Don't be shy!" He pulled her over and handed her a ruby from a giant pile.

Laura and Quin looked on nervously, their minds racing through the ten thousand ways this could go horribly wrong.

Tortle got the other goblins chanting, "Ruby Toss! Ruby Toss! Ruby Toss!"

Millie wound up and balanced on her back foot, trying to gather all her strength. Then she heaved the heavy ruby as hard as she could straight at the chalice—or so she thought. It quickly veered off course and sailed right into the head of a nearby goblin, knocking him out cold.

Tortle and his friends gasped as the goblin hit the floor. For a long moment, they stared at Millie in stunned silence. It looked as though they were about to chomp her to bits with their needle teeth. Millie started sweating with fear, trying to figure out if she should scream, run, or both.

Tortle grabbed Millie's wrist. He held her hand up in the air. "The new champion!" he bellowed. His friends jumped and cheered.

Millie let out a huge sigh of relief.

"That was way better than our game!" said one of the goblins.

"My favorite part was when she hit him in the head with the ruby!" said another.

"Mine too!" said a third.

Tortle scooped up an armful of gold from the ground and handed it to Millie. She stumbled away, awkwardly trying not to drop all the coins.

"Phew!" she said to Laura. "Who knew I had such good aim?"

As they wandered deeper into the goblin party, there was no sign of the Crystal Crown or the throne room that they had seen in the basin of water at Deirdre's. Laura spotted a narrow tunnel at the far end of the cavern. It was aglow with goblin wax candles.

Laura nodded toward it. "Over there."

To get to the tunnel, they needed to push through the horde of goblins at the foot of the stage. Goblin dancing was mostly elbows, which made the journey treacherous. They ducked and swerved their way through the crowd and were almost to the other side when the screeching music came

to an abrupt stop. The accordion player called out, "It's the moment you've all been waiting for. Time for the Gobtrot!"

The goblins cheered and instantly formed an enormous circle, holding hands. Before they could escape, Laura, Millie, Quin, and Donkeycorn were grabbed and brought into the formation. The band broke out in a fast-paced song, and the goblins walked in a circle, crisscrossing their feet. Donkeycorn nearly tripped and fell with every step, but Laura and Millie just managed to hold him up.

The accordion player shouted, "Couples trot!"

As the circle kept on moving, pairs of goblins took turns jumping into the center to perform their own take on the Gobtrot. An old couple hopped from one foot to the other and stuck their elbows out to the sides, their stringy white hair whipping every which way.

Suddenly Laura felt goblin hands on her back as she and Quin were pushed into the middle of the circle.

Laura could see the panic in Quin's eyes.

"What do we do?" he said under his breath.

"I don't know! What do I look like, a goblin?" she whispered.

"Actually, yes! We all look like goblins!"

With nowhere to hide, they tried their best to imitate the dancing. But right away, goblins from the circle shouted their disapproval.

"What's wrong with these two? Stick your elbows out farther!"

"Your knees should be hitting your forehead!"

Laura and Quin tried to follow the instructions, but the harder they danced, the more they just looked like confused chickens.

Thankfully, another goblin couple jumped in, and they were able to slink away. While the two goblins in the middle wowed the crowd by kicking their filthy feet high above their heads, Laura and Quin grabbed Millie and Donkeycorn and slipped out of the circle. As they left, a goblin with a wart-covered face reached out and took Donkeycorn's hand. "Care to couples trot?"

Donkeycorn grinned and started to respond, "Hee—"

But before he could say "haw," Laura interrupted, "He's not feeling too well."

The warty goblin slumped his shoulders and walked away, disappointed.

They finally made it to the tunnel. As they crept down it, the sounds of the party behind them became muffled and quiet. The goblin candles were spaced farther apart on the wall, so the tunnel grew darker and darker. They reached a point where it split in two directions.

"Which way?" Millie whispered.

From the left, they heard a low rumbling. They followed the sound and had barely taken a few steps when they saw shimmers of silver and glints of gold. At the end of the tunnel was the throne room, just as they had seen it in the basin—the piles of precious jewels, the long table with the ruby-encrusted box, and in the center, a golden throne.

Slouched on the throne in a deep sleep was the largest goblin of them all, at least three times the size of the others. The Crystal Crown was perched on his head.

Laura's blood felt like ice in her veins. "Bloato."

Laura couldn't believe it! She had a clear path to the crown. All she had to do was run up and take it.

Take it back.

Before even realizing what she was doing, Laura left Millie and Quin behind and ran down the tunnel as fast as she could. She heard her goblin feet slapping against the cold ground. She reached the throne room and skidded to a stop. She tiptoed toward Bloato silently. He was snoring so loudly, it sounded like there was a whole choir of frogs lodged in the back of his throat. A thick strand of drool leaked from the corner of his mouth onto his swollen belly.

She reached out slowly, carefully, toward the crown. She could see the warm flicker of the goblin candlelight reflected in its surface. She could feel the ancient power of Lysoria compelling her to snatch it off Bloato's thieving head. Her fingertips were inches away, when—

Ding! Ding! Ding!

The harsh sound of a bell clanged throughout the entire cave so loud, it pierced the insides of Laura's pointy goblin ears.

Bloato's eyes snapped open.

LAURA FROZE IN TERROR as Bloato groggily wiped his crusty eyes. He looked curiously at the goblin standing before him.

Laura said the first thing that popped into her head. "Good morning! I mean—good afternoon! I mean—good evening?"

Bloato let out a groan and cleared his throat. "Is it feasting hour?"

"Uh . . . yes?" Laura said meekly.

Bloato cracked his neck. It sounded like twigs popping in a fire. He pushed himself up out of his throne and went over to the long table with the ruby-encrusted box, his bloated belly jiggling with every step. He grabbed the gold silk tablecloth and yanked it toward him, sending the jeweled box crashing to the ground. He brought it to his nose and blew with a *honk* like an angry goose. The shimmering gold threads were covered in thick green mucus.

"That's better," he said, his voice like curdled milk. Without a second thought, he tossed the cloth at Laura, and it landed on her head. She quickly pulled it off, trying her best not to gag.

Just then, two goblins hurried into the throne room. "It's feasting hour, King Bloato!" said the first goblin.

"About time," Bloato huffed.

"Yes, it's been a long three hours since the last feast. We've missed you!" said the second goblin.

The goblins took Bloato's arms and led him out of the room.

"I was dreaming of salty cheeses," said Bloato.

"Well, sir, if anyone can make dreams come true, it's you!" The first goblin turned around and snapped at Laura, "Don't just stand there. Fetch his chalice!"

Laura dropped the snot-covered cloth and scrambled over to the throne, where a silver chalice was resting on a small side table. She watched the goblins usher Bloato away, all the while never taking her eyes off the Crystal Crown on his head.

She followed them down the tunnel. When she reached the point where the tunnel split in two directions, Millie popped out.

"Did you get it?" she whispered. She and Quin had been hiding around the corner, along with Donkeycorn.

Laura shook her head. "I was so close! Then that stupid bell rang."

"What's the plan now?" asked Quin.

"The plan?" Laura said. "Go to a goblin feast."

When they got back to the enormous cavern, four long tables had been arranged in a square with a seat for every goblin. The tables were decorated with the same gold-spun cloths that Bloato had just used as a handkerchief, along with goblin wax candles in glittering candelabras. There was a silver plate carved with an ornate pattern at every seat, except Bloato's—which had a golden platter large enough to fit a whole week's worth of Lysor rations.

Laura headed straight for Bloato, holding the chalice. As she neared the crown, she felt electricity surge inside her. She thought about grabbing it right off his wrinkly head and making a run for it, but before she could reach him, one of his goblin servants stepped in front of her.

"I'll take that!" he said, snatching the chalice from her hands. "Now, sit down!" He rushed over to Bloato and placed the chalice in front of him with a bow.

The seats were filling up fast. Laura, Millie, Quin, and Donkeycorn squeezed into the only chairs they could find.

Quin looked around at the empty plates, confused. "I thought this was a feast. Where's all the food?"

"Wherever it is, I hope it's not raw onion," said Millie.

"Let's just get through this, and then we'll make our move," said Laura.

"Hee—" said Donkeycorn.

"Shh!" said Laura.

Bloato pounded his enormous fist on the table, and plates rattled. The entire cavern fell silent. He raised his silver chalice in the air. The crown atop his head glowed so brightly that everyone had to shield their eyes. Through the blinding light, Bloato called out, "Let the goblin feast begin!" When the light faded, the table was covered in enormous piles of food.

The goblins let out a raucous cheer and began heaping food onto their plates. They tore off roasted turkey legs with their bare hands. They dug their fingers into mountains of pungent cheese and slurped from enormous bowls of creamy soups. Bloato picked up a platinum pitcher of gravy and poured it straight down his throat.

Donkeycorn shoved his face into a dish of buttery potatoes. For a moment, Laura was certain Donkeycorn was going to get them caught. But when the goblins sitting near him saw how quickly he could chomp down his food, they all did the same. They seemed to think that was the best idea in the world.

"Forget finger food," said one of the goblins. "This is face food!" He sunk his teeth into a glistening ham without even bothering to take it off the serving platter.

Trying her best to fit in, Laura filled her plate with handfuls of sausages, beans, and chicken livers. She ate distractedly, all the while racking her brain for a way to get to the crown.

Meanwhile, Millie and Quin were feasting as enthusiastically as everyone else at the table.

Millie took a big gulp of chunky soup. "Whatever is in here, I have to add it to my Thew."

Quin bit into a leg of lamb and closed his eyes, savoring the taste. "This is even better than beetle butts."

The serving platters were starting to empty, but the goblins showed no signs of stopping.

Bloato pounded his fist on the table again. "Time for seconds!" he shouted. There was another bright flash of light from the Crystal Crown, and instantly, the table was as full of food as it had been at the beginning of the feast.

The goblins dug in with even more vigor. Juices and grease dribbled down their chins, and saliva flew from their mouths in all directions. The buttons on their vests started to strain against their bellies.

Laura started to feel sick, and it wasn't just because of the oily chicken livers. The Crystal Crown was powerful beyond the strongest mind. She couldn't bear seeing that power being wasted like this.

Quin pushed his plate away. "I never thought I'd say this, but I can't eat another bite."

"Me neither," said Millie, looking anxiously at the endless spread of food.

Even Donkeycorn looked a little overwhelmed.

Bloato put his hand on his stomach and leaned back in his chair, breathing heavily. "I haven't been this full since breakfast." He looked as though he might finally be finished. But then he banged his fist on the table and shouted, "Dessert!"

With another blinding flash of light, the food that was left on the table vanished, and in its place appeared heaps of pastries, pies stuffed with every fruit imaginable, and cakes with so many layers, they towered above the goblins' heads.

Millie turned to Laura, looking a little ill. "It's got to stop soon, right?"

Quin looked around at the goblins gorging on the sweets and washing them down with jugs of thick cream. "I wouldn't count on it."

Bloato was holding a stick of butter as big as his own arm. He dipped it in a bowl of sugar and then shoved the whole thing in his mouth. He clapped his hands and demanded, "More merriment!"

The room was filled with shouts of "Hear, hear!" and "Great idea, King Bloato!"

The servant at Bloato's side grabbed a candle from its holder on the table and held it high. "Let's play Wax the Candle!"

A huge smile crept across Bloato's face. Butter oozed between his needle teeth. "Yes, Wax the Candle it is. Winner gets a prize!" With a flash of the Crystal Crown, a pile of gold as tall as a tree appeared beside him.

The goblins cheered so loudly and wildly, Laura was afraid the chandeliers were going to come crashing down from the ceiling. She turned to Quin. "What's Wax the Candle?"

Quin shrugged. "I think we're about to find out."

Bloato's servant went first. He placed the lumpy black candle on the table in front of him. Then he stuck his finger in his pointy ear, deeper than it looked like a finger should be able to go. When he pulled his finger back out, it was covered in a thick glob of black earwax. He stuck it on the side of the candle.

Millie let out a low groan. "I guess we know how goblin wax candles are made."

Laura shuddered, thinking about how much goblin earwax it must have taken to make the candles lighting the entire cave.

The candle was passed to the next goblin, who crammed her finger into her ear.

"I can beat that!" she sneered. She dug around inside and pulled out an even bigger mound of goop. The first goblin put his head on the table in disappointment. The candle was passed around the table, and one by one, the goblins competed to see who could mine the most wax from their ear canals. By the time it reached Laura, the candle was three times its original size and a thousand times more disgusting.

She turned to Millie. "Here goes," she said under her breath. She could hardly believe what she was about to do, but she had no choice. She stuck her finger in her ear, hoping to pull out a glob and get her turn over with as fast as possible.

But what she found was even more stomach churning than a lump of goblin earwax.

Nothing.

All the goblin eyes were on her. "Uh . . . let me try the other ear," she said.

But her other ear was empty, too. Suddenly it dawned on her. The Chamelixir made her look like a goblin on the outside. But inside, she was all Lysor—and that, apparently, included the inside of her ear.

Bloato was frowning so deeply that the corners of his mouth drooped all the way down to his chin. "You," he beckoned. "Come."

Laura slowly pushed her chair back. Millie grabbed on to her wrist, her eyes urging Laura not to go. But Laura shook her off. She picked up the candle and walked toward Bloato. With every step she took, she grew more fearful. She stopped just inches away from Bloato. The Crystal Crown sparkled atop his head.

He took the candle from her and placed it on the table in front of him. He narrowed his eyes at her. "I've never seen a goblin with empty ears before."

Laura could feel her throat getting dry. "I, uh . . . must have just cleaned them."

Bloato looked at her incredulously. "*Cleaned* your *ears*?"

The goblins turned to each other, whispering, "I've

never cleaned my ears in my life" and "What a waste of perfectly good wax."

"You know what I think?" Bloato leaned in closer to Laura. "I think you're not a goblin *at all*!" He pounded his fist on the table with such force that a stalactite fell from the ceiling.

Millie leaped up from her chair. "Run, Laura!"

Bloato's face twisted in anger. "Laura?"

Laura knew it was now or never. With her eyes fixed on the crown, she said, "Tier'e."

Instantly, the Chamelixir's enchantment was broken by the use of Lysor magic. Laura, Millie, Quin, and Donkeycorn transformed back into their regular bodies.

At the same time, the flame from the goblin wax candle flared up, and the candle exploded, sending globs of black wax in all directions. The force sent Bloato toppling off his chair. He hit the ground with a loud *thud*. The crown fell off his head and rolled across the floor.

"Laura, get it!" Quin shouted, pointing at the crown.

"Seize them!" Bloato's servant screeched.

The goblins ran toward them, baring their needle teeth.

Laura dove to the ground and crawled under the table. She saw the crown glittering beneath a chair. She scrambled over to it and reached out to grab it, but then Bloato's servant stepped on her hand with his hairy goblin foot.

"Gotcha," he said with a grin.

Dozens of goblin hands seized Laura, Millie, Quin, and

Donkeycorn and hauled them toward the back of the cavern. Bloato's servants hoisted him back onto his chair and placed the crown back on his head.

"Wait." Bloato pointed at Donkeycorn. "Bring me the beast."

The goblins walked Donkeycorn over, and Bloato patted him on the back. "We'll have him for the next feast."

"No!" Laura screamed, but she couldn't be heard over the uproarious goblin cheering.

The goblins hauled them down the tunnel. At the point where it split in two directions, they went away from the throne room, where there was a metal grate in the ground above a deep, dark hole. The goblins unlocked the grate and threw them down, down, down, into the darkness.

THE DUNGEON DEEP BENEATH the goblin cave was ice-cold. The light streaming through the grate above was so dim, Laura could barely see her hand in front of her. It was the darkest place she had ever been in her life, she realized, because for the first time ever, her green lock wasn't glowing at all.

"Laura, are you okay?" Millie called from a few feet away.

"I think so." Laura made her way over to Millie and saw that her lock wasn't glowing, either.

"I wish I was still a goblin," said Quin, rubbing his ribs. "That big belly could have broken my fall."

"There's got to be a way out of here," said Laura. "We need some light."

"On it." Quin pushed himself up. "Tier'e!" he said. He struck his thumb and forefinger together to start a fire, but nothing happened. Not even a spark. He tried again. And then again. "It's not working." There was a twinge of panic in his voice, like a soldier who had lost his sword.

Millie shivered. "We'll freeze to death down here! Or die of thirst! Or get eaten by some . . . weird cave monster!"

"Millie, calm down! I have an idea," Laura said firmly. She rummaged around in her rucksack and pulled out a page of enchanted parchment. "My dad will help us. If we can tell him how to get here, he'll make sure all the Lysors come and save us." She quickly began writing.

Dad,
Something terrible has happened. We need your help.
We're trapped beneath the goblin c . . .

But Laura saw that as she wrote, the ink wasn't glowing. The enchantment wasn't working. It was just a piece of ordinary parchment paper. Laura was writing to no one but herself.

Millie gasped in horror. "None of our magic works down here!" She started pacing. "All magic—Lysor, Hexor, small mage—it all comes from the same source: the moons. Lysoria and Hexia. We're trapped so far away from them that we'll never be able to use our magic to get out of here!"

Laura clenched her jaw. "We'll find a way. We were so close to the Crystal Crown—"

"But now we couldn't be farther away!" Millie cried. "And unless you know how to climb up stone walls and break open a locked grate with your bare hands, we don't have a chance!"

"Now is not the time to panic," Laura seethed.

"It's the perfect time to panic!"

Laura exploded, "Millie, for you, every time is the perfect time to panic! And every time you do, it makes things worse! Why did you have to say my name in front of Bloato? You gave us away!"

"*I* gave us away?!" Millie shouted. "You were the one who used magic and ruined our disguise! Why do you always jump headfirst into everything without ever thinking?"

"*Here's* what I think," Laura snapped. "I think you shouldn't have come with me in the first place!"

Millie sniffled. Even in the darkness, Laura could tell that she was fighting back tears. "You do?" Millie whispered.

Quin held up his hands. "It's not anybody's fault we're down here."

Laura turned on him. "Oh really? Maybe it's your fault! I thought you were supposed to protect us. All you've done is make us eat beetle butts!"

"It's not my fault the butt is the most nutritious part of the beetle!"

"I don't care!" Laura yelled.

"Laura, calm down," Quin said.

"Calm down?! That's easy for you to say. You're not out

here trying to save your home and your family. You don't even have a family to save."

Quin bit his lip. He took a deep breath. "If we're ever going to get out of here, we need to work together."

"That's the last thing I need to do," Laura scoffed. She ran her hands along the smooth rock wall and felt an opening just big enough to fit through. "I'm going to find a way out of here. Alone." She climbed through the opening, leaving Millie and Quin behind.

She found herself at the edge of a long tunnel with no end in sight. Without much of anything in sight, actually. As she put one foot in front of the other, it got darker and darker until it quickly became pitch-black. She walked and walked, touching her fingertips to the side of the tunnel. It twisted and turned, leading her deeper into the darkness. She tried to keep her mind off the cold wrapping itself around her like a blanket of ice. But then all she could think about was the Crystal Crown sitting on Bloato's crusty head for all eternity. She was haunted by thoughts of the Hexors marching toward Hillview, preparing to rot away the only home she'd ever known. She felt foolish for ever wanting to leave and wished more than anything that she could be back there right at this moment. And the worst thought of all lodged itself in the forefront of her mind—she would never see her dad again.

Laura felt the tunnel branching out in all different directions. She had no idea how long she had been walking.

But she knew one thing—she was completely and totally lost. Once again, she found herself surrounded by walls. But this time, there were no cracks to look through. And there was no Millie to comfort her.

Laura slid down to the ground. She had destroyed the only true friendship she had ever had. Of course she had wanted Millie to come with her. She needed Millie. And she needed Quin, too. She wiped the tears from her eyes and shouted as loud as she could, *"I'm sorry!"* Maybe it was impossible for them to hear her, but she had to try. "I need you! Both of you! I can't do this alone!"

She put her head in her hands and sobbed. It was so dark, she couldn't even tell if her eyes were open. Suddenly, between her short breaths, she heard footsteps echoing through the tunnel. And they were getting closer.

A soft, raspy voice called out, "Hello?"

It wasn't Millie. It wasn't Quin. It was a voice Laura didn't recognize.

The frail voice called out again. "Is—is someone there?"

Laura trembled, trying to stay quiet, but the sound of her breathing gave her away.

"It's okay. I won't hurt you," said the voice, right next to her now.

Laura whimpered, "I'm lost. I need to find my friends."

"I can help you," said the voice. "I know my way around these tunnels."

"How can you know the way?" Laura asked. "It's so dark."

"I've been trapped down here for eleven years."

Eleven years.

A heap of puzzle pieces in Laura's mind suddenly snapped themselves into place.

Eleven years.

Laura scrambled to her feet. "Mom?"

"LAURA?" THE VOICE SAID, cracking with emotion. It *was* her mom.

"Yes! Yes, it's me!" said Laura.

Reina scooped Laura up into a hug that warmed Laura to the core. She wrapped her arms around her mother's neck. Suddenly it all made sense. *Bloato wears the Crystal Crown* was the last thing Reina wrote because it was the last thing she *could* write. The enchanted parchment was useless down here. And when Deirdre had shown Laura the view through her mother's eyes, she couldn't see anything because she was staring at the darkness of the tunnels beneath the goblin cave. As her mother squeezed her tightly, Laura felt at home for the first time since leaving Hillview.

"How did you survive down here for so long?" Laura asked.

"Every few days, the goblins toss down scraps of food

through the grate," Reina explained. "These tunnels are the only place I can get away from that terrible goblin music. You can only hear the Gobtrot so many times before it drives you crazy."

"That's it!" said Laura. "The room with the grate. Can you get me back there? That's where my friends are." Laura paused. "If they're even my friends anymore. They probably hate me now."

"Just tell them how you feel," said Reina. "If there's one thing I learned being trapped down here, it's never miss a chance to tell someone how much they mean to you."

Laura held Reina's hand tightly as Reina led her through the tunnels. Laura explained everything she could about Hillview and the Hexors, about Millie and Quin. Just as she was telling Reina that her notebook was the reason they'd found her in the first place, she saw dim light up ahead. In the room underneath the grate, Millie was huddled in the corner, her knees to her chest. Quin was trying unsuccessfully to climb up the side of the rock wall.

"Millie!" Laura called.

Millie leaped up. "Laura, is that you?"

Laura ran to her. "Millie, I'm so sorry," she said. "You're my best friend! I don't know what I'd do without you! I wouldn't have made it over the first hill, and I definitely wouldn't have made it past that horrible troll!" She turned to Quin. "And, Quin, if it wasn't for you, a rotslobber would have torn me to pieces! I'm so sorry for what I said. You've risked your life for us over and over again. If that's not family, I don't know what is. Can you two ever forgive me?"

Millie and Quin looked at each other.

Quin grinned. "Does a goblin have black earwax?"

They both wrapped up Laura in a big hug. That's when they saw Reina standing behind her.

Laura turned around. For the first time since she was a baby, Laura could finally see her mom. In the dim light, she saw how much her mother looked like her—the wide curious eyes, the jet-black hair—except Reina's was so long, it hung all the way down to her waist.

"Millicent! By all the moons in the sky!" Reina smiled. "How's my favorite niece?"

Millie had never looked so confused in her life. "Aunt Reina?"

"I got lost, and she found me," said Laura.

Reina put her hand on Laura's shoulder. "We found each other."

"This is our friend Quin," said Laura.

"He helped us get a Donkeycorn!" said Millie.

Reina arched her eyebrow. "I can see I've missed a lot."

"More than you could ever know, Mom," said Laura. "But right now we have to find a way out of here."

Reina frowned. "I've spent years wandering these tunnels. There's no way out."

Millie pointed to the grate. "Maybe we can hoist each other up or, I don't know, stand on each other's shoulders!"

Laura shook her head. "Millie, that grate has to be twenty feet up. There's only four of us."

Quin gasped. "Four of us! There's four of us down here!"

Laura sighed. "Yes, Quin, we all can count."

"You don't understand!" said Quin, a wild look in his eye. He opened Laura's rucksack and pulled out the book from Hobbly Knobbly. He frantically flipped through it until he found the page he was looking for. "An Elemental Tornado!" He pointed to the page and read, "'In times when Lysor power was compromised, four Lysors could create an Elemental Tornado by summoning all the elements at once. It must be four Lysors—no more, no less!'"

Laura looked to Reina. "Do you think that could work?"

"It might. But it's too risky. In an Elemental Tornado, the elements combine in unpredictable ways. You never quite know what you're going to get. It must be done with four Lysors. A small mage might not survive."

Quin took a step forward. "I've wrestled rotslobbers. I've outrun scabengers. I've tasted Hobbly Knobbly's bathwater. You'd be surprised what I can survive."

"You don't understand the power of an Elemental Tornado," said Reina.

"Maybe I don't," said Quin, "but all I've done my whole life is fend for myself. Now I have the chance to help you all get out of here and to save the Lysors." He turned to Laura. "Let me do this for you. Please."

Laura could tell, looking into his green and violet eyes, that he wasn't going to take no for an answer. "You're sure?"

Without so much as a moment of hesitation, he said, "Yes."

They all turned to Reina.

"Then let's begin," she said.

They stood in a circle, and Reina told each of them which element they would be summoning. She would summon earth, Laura air, Millie water, and Quin, of course, fire.

"Join hands," Reina commanded.

Laura felt heat surging from her mother's firm grip on one side and Quin's papery palm on the other. Across the circle, she saw Millie looking braver than she ever had before. Laura knew they were far from the moon of Lysoria, but she hoped the power of the four elements was enough. Reina nodded, then they all closed their eyes.

Their voices echoed in unison:

"Talamh'e," said Reina.

"Goith'e," said Laura.

"Tier'e," said Quin.

"Oighar'e," said Millie.

Laura's palms burned so hot, she felt as if she had grabbed a pot from a fire with her bare hands. But she held on tight.

The earth began to shake beneath them. Then suddenly the ground split open with a *crack!* so loud that Millie nearly jumped out of her skin. Out of the ground gushed a massive geyser of water, swirling like a tornado, encircled in flames.

It all happened in a second, but as the geyser erupted underneath them, time seemed to slow down. Laura felt the air whipping upward, lifting them toward the metal grate. She felt the cool spray of water on her skin, protecting them from the fire. She saw the white-hot flames lick the grate, instantly melting it away.

Then, all at once, they were spat up onto the ground of the goblin cave as if a wave had washed them onto a deserted island. The icy water crashed back down to the floor of the dungeon, where it seeped through the cracks and disappeared. As quickly as the Elemental Tornado had begun, it was over.

Laura scrambled to her feet. "It worked! It really worked!" she said, panting like she'd just sprinted for miles.

She helped up Millie, who looked a little dizzy. "Did that actually just happen?" Millie asked in a daze.

"Yes!" Laura said, laughing. But her joy was short-lived, as she saw Reina lifting up Quin in her arms. Laura ran to him and held his head. He was breathing, but his eyes were closed and his body was limp as he drifted in and out of consciousness.

"He doesn't have long," Reina said gravely.

That's when they heard the *"DING! DING! DING!"* of the feast bell.

Millie gasped. "Donkeycorn!"

LAURA AND MILLIE RAN through the tunnel as fast as they could, Reina carrying Quin behind them. When they reached the split in the tunnel, they could see at the other end that the throne room was empty.

"Bloato must already be at the feast," said Laura.

"Let's go!" said Millie urgently.

They turned down the tunnel that led to the main cavern. Donkeycorn was just up ahead. There was a rope tied around his horn, and one of Bloato's servants was pulling him forward. Donkeycorn dug his hooves into the ground stubbornly and let out a nervous bray.

"Come *on*!" Bloato's servant grunted, yanking the rope. "And get that stupid grin off your face, you're about to be dinner!"

Laura turned to her mom. "How are we going to free him? Is there some kind of Lysor magic we can—"

But before she could finish her sentence, Millie was

running at full speed toward the servant, shouting, *"That's my Donkeycorn!"*

As the servant turned in surprise, Millie punched him square in the jaw so hard that black earwax flew out of his ears, and he fell to the ground in a heap.

"Millie!" Laura exclaimed, her mouth agape. "How did you do that?"

Millie rubbed her fist, wincing in pain. "I didn't lug around thirty pounds of gray pears every week for nothing."

Donkeycorn gave Millie the biggest grin he had ever grinned in his whole life. It looked ridiculous.

Laura and Millie hopped onto Donkeycorn's back. Reina lifted Quin on, then climbed up behind him. It was a tight squeeze, but there was just enough room on Donkeycorn's rotund rump for all of them.

There was a flash of white light, and Bloato's voice echoed through the cave. "Let the goblin feast begin!"

Reina shuddered. "I've heard him say that six times a day for the last eleven years. I don't want to hear it ever again."

Laura turned back and said, "Then let's make sure it's the last time."

Laura steered Donkeycorn a few steps forward so she could just see the goblins gathered around the tables, salivating at the massive piles of food. They were about to dig in when Bloato banged his fist on the table.

"Wait!" he bellowed. "We'll start with our special first course . . . Donkeycorn!"

The goblins clapped and cheered as Bloato leaned back in his chair, smiling with satisfaction. But then they saw Laura riding Donkeycorn in a full gallop across the cavern straight toward Bloato, her eyes fixed on the Crystal Crown. Millie hung on to Laura's back. Reina clung to Millie with one hand and held up Quin with the other. All the goblins gasped in utter shock as Laura snatched the crown right off Bloato's head.

The goblins erupted in outrage. They sprang up from their chairs and chased after Donkeycorn, who was running at top speed. Bloato banged his fist on the table over and over again, wailing in anger, causing so many stalactites to crash down from the ceiling that Laura was afraid they'd be crushed. She could feel the power of the Crystal Crown surging through her body like a bolt of lightning. As Donkeycorn dodged the falling rocks and the mob of goblins, Laura was jolted from side to side, and she nearly lost her grip on the crown. She couldn't risk dropping it. She stuck the crown on the safest place she could see—right on Donkeycorn's head. As soon as the crown encircled his horn, there was a blinding flash of light. Donkeycorn took a mighty leap and soared up into the air.

"Donkeycorn!" Millie shouted. "You can fly!"

It was a bit of an overstatement—Donkeycorn was barely high enough to fly up onto the banquet table. He landed clumsily, his front hoof squashing a turkey to smithereens. He galloped across the table, smashing the potatoes and kicking over bowls of creamy soups. They were headed straight for Bloato, who managed to push himself up from his seat.

"Stop them!" Bloato shouted.

As Donkeycorn reached the edge of the table, he took flight again, just high enough that the bottom of his belly grazed the top of Bloato's wrinkled, bald head. He flew around in lopsided loops like a confused baby bird, knocking over piles of gemstones and sending gold and silver coins skittering across the ground.

The goblins ran around beneath him trying to jump up and grab his hooves. But Donkeycorn gained control of his new power and flew even higher, heading toward the entrance of the cave. As Donkeycorn carried the crown farther and farther from Bloato's reach, all the food on the table turned to dust. The goblins cried out in anguish as their once-bountiful feast blew away into nothing. Then the gold, the silver, and all the gems melted into shimmering liquid and oozed across the ground.

Bloato let out a tortured roar as he tried to scoop up the remnants of the treasures, but the melted metal slipped through his sausage-like fingers and disappeared through the cracks in the cave floor.

Donkeycorn sailed through the front tunnel. Laura could see the evening light of the outside world up ahead. At the sight of it, Reina let out a soft gasp of wonder. They flew out of the cave, then Laura turned back and shouted, "Goith'e!"

A great wind blew through the cave, extinguishing every last black candle and plunging the goblins into darkness. She smiled and nodded to her mom. "Your turn."

"Talamh'e!" said Reina, making a fist. The cave entrance crumbled, sealing the goblins inside forever, as Donkeycorn soared up into the sky.

"WE DID IT! WE actually did it!" Laura cheered as Donkeycorn flew through the air.

Laura and Millie held on tight as the cold evening wind whipped through their hair. Reina held Quin steady. His breathing was shallow, and his face was pale.

The shimmering crown was still firmly placed on Donkeycorn's head. He swooped through the vast canyons gracefully, with a big dumb smile on his face, of course. When he made a sharp turn around the edge of a cliff, his motion sickness kicked in, and without warning, he puked. But this time, instead of vomiting up whatever Hobbly Knobbly had been feeding him, a rainbow shot out of his mouth at the speed of light, covering the ground beneath them in brilliant colors.

"Yay!" Millie cheered. "He really does have all the magic of a unicorn!"

"Hee-haw!" Donkeycorn brayed.

"And all the powers of a donkey!" she added.

Millie tugged on Laura's shoulder. "Look!" she said, pointing behind them.

The moons were rising in the east, but Laura stayed focused on the setting sun up ahead. She watched it dip below the horizon.

"The Hexor army must be close to Hillview by now," said Laura.

"If they're not there already," Millie fretted.

"We don't have to be afraid anymore," said Laura. "We have the crown now. Once we make it home, we'll be able to lock up the Hexors back where they came from. Forever."

"Go that way," Reina said, pointing to the left, where there was a gap in the mountains. "I need to show you something."

"But, Mom—"

"Trust me," Reina said in a tone only a mom knows how to use. A tone Laura hadn't heard in a very long time. "There's something you need to see."

Laura steered Donkeycorn through the gap in the mountains. Suddenly a smell hit her like a punch to the nose—a curdling odor that crawled up her nostrils and refused to leave. Rot. Mold. Decay. As Donkeycorn flew, the smell got worse and worse. It became unbearable as they reached a vast thicket of dead trees covered in razor-sharp thorns. The trees glowed violet, and their branches were twisted and bent, overlapping to form an enormous wooden cage—an impenetrable fortress of rot.

Laura realized where her mom had steered them. "The Putrid Forest," she said with a grimace.

Millie held her arm in front of her nose, her eyes watering from the stench. "Why would you take us here?!"

"Because I need you to understand," said Reina. "Years ago, when I was out exploring, I found this place. No Lysor had been here for centuries. Of course, I had heard that the Putrid Forest was terrible. But actually *seeing* it. *Smelling* it. That was different. And we Lysors trapped the Hexors here for hundreds of years."

"But the Hexors are the reason it's so horrible," said Millie. "They're so rotten to the core that they turned the whole forest rotten!"

Reina shook her head.

"You mean, we were lied to?" said Laura.

"Not exactly . . . ," said Reina, searching for the right words as they soared over gnarled, tangled branches. "We lied to *ourselves.* The Hexors didn't make this forest putrid. The Lysors did. We imprisoned them in a cage of death and rot."

Laura looked down. She saw rotslobbers running wild, drooling and snarling. Scabengers preened their sickly feathers in enormous nests made of dead twigs.

Reina continued, "When I returned from my expedition, I told Queen Ailix what I had seen. She was horrified. That's why she freed the Hexors."

"Queen Ailix freed the Hexors because of *you*?" Laura said breathlessly.

Reina nodded. "She was a good queen."

They reached the edge of the forest, where there was a break in the cage of trees.

Laura was beginning to understand. She knew the feeling of being trapped all too well. "The Hexors were desperate and starving. Of course they hated the Lysors."

Reina nodded. "We made them the monsters that we're now afraid of."

"But this can't be!" Millie cried. "The Lysors are good! Lysoria was the good twin! Hexia was evil!"

"That's what the Lysors say," said Reina. "But the Hexors say that Lysoria was the evil twin."

Laura and Millie were so stunned that they were speechless. Everything they had ever been taught in school, everything they had been told about who the Lysors were, who the Hexors were, had been wrong.

"If we banish the Hexors again, the cycle will just continue," said Reina. "It's already gone on for far, far too long."

"Then we won't banish them," said Laura. "The Crystal Crown is powerful beyond the strongest mind. It must be powerful enough to finally make peace."

By the time they approached the Dead End, the sky was completely dark except for the light of the moons. Up ahead, they saw smoke rising from the chimneys of the small clay homes. As they neared Hobbly Knobbly's house, Donkeycorn swerved toward it, braying excitedly.

"Whoa, Donkeycorn!" Laura called out, trying to steer him toward the hills.

But Donkeycorn had his own ideas. He circled Hobbly's front yard. Suddenly the Crystal Crown on his head flashed with light, and the carved bushes were set ablaze with a dazzling green glow.

"Donkeycorn, what are you doing?" Laura urged.

"He wants to go home," said Millie.

Laura patted Donkeycorn's neck. "Hang in there, buddy. We need you to get us to Hillview first."

Donkeycorn flew over the Dead End and up the steep incline that led into the hills. He coasted between the trees, toward the valley where their home was hidden. But when he crested the final hill, Laura's heart sank. There was Hillview in plain sight. The enchantment had been broken. All four walls had collapsed into heaps of smoldering rubble. Glowing locks of hair—green and violet—whipped around in chaos.

The Hexors had invaded.

As they flew closer, they saw the Hexors rampaging through Hillview. They rode their horses through the Never-Dark Forest, shooting enchanted arrows into every tree trunk. One by one, the trees turned violet, then shriveled and died. The Hexors demolished the Lysor homes, their arrows crumbling the walls to the ground. They dug through the rubble, leaving no stone unturned in the search for the crown. They spat wads of black saliva into the Clear Lake, causing the water to turn a sickly brown and dead fish to rise to the surface. The Endless Well bubbled and boiled with black steam rising high into the air. Lysors ran in every direction, trying to stay out of the Hexors' path of destruction.

The chaos came to an abrupt stop as the Hexors and Lysors spotted Donkeycorn flying overhead, the Crystal Crown shining on his horn. Their eyes went wide and their jaws dropped, black ooze dribbling from the Hexors' mouths.

Laura steered Donkeycorn to the Food-Giving Tree. They landed underneath its wide-reaching branches, heavy with gray pears. They leaped off Donkeycorn. Reina set Quin down in the grass.

Micah made it to them first.

"Dad!" Laura shouted.

"Laura!" he cried, wrapping his arms around her. "I was so worried!"

"You worry too much," said Reina from behind him.

When he turned around and saw her, he shook his head as if he were waking up from a strange dream. "Reina? Is that really you?"

Reina nodded, her eyes brimming with happy tears.

Micah hugged her tightly. "I thought you were lost forever."

"So did I," she whispered. "I'll explain everything. But first, you have to save this boy. He's slipping away."

Micah knelt down next to Quin, whose breathing was more shallow than ever. Micah's face steeled in determination. "It's somewhere in the rubble," he muttered. Then he tore off toward the ruins of his collapsed home.

"Laura," Millie squeaked, tugging on her sleeve. "Look."

Laura saw the Hexors closing in around her. As they surrounded the Food-Giving Tree, Laura took the Crystal Crown off Donkeycorn's head. The Hexors drew their arrows all at once.

At the front of the pack was Erika, Hugo at her side. The tip of her arrow was pointed directly at Laura's heart.

"Hand over the crown," Erika commanded.

"No," Laura said firmly.

"Fine." Erika shrugged. "I'll take it myself."

She let her arrow fly.

LAURA LEAPED OUT OF the arrow's path just in time. She could feel the violet feathers graze her arm before the arrow hit the Food-Giving Tree. The tree glowed violet, then rot crept out from the site of the puncture. The trunk grew soft and moldy. The branches began to twist. The leaves dried up. The gray pears rotted and fell to the ground like heavy black raindrops.

The Hexors all looked to Erika.

"Hold your fire. This one's mine," she said, beckoning her arrow to return to her.

Torian pushed his way through the crowd. "Laura!" he called. "Use the power of the crown! Send them back to the Putrid Forest, where they belong!"

Erika scrambled to reload her arrow into her bow. Laura thought she spotted a glimpse of fear in her eyes.

"That's not what I came here to do," Laura said, gripping the crown so tightly that the crystal almost cut into her palm. She turned to Erika. "What the Lysors did, trapping you in that horrible forest . . . it was wrong."

A flash of surprise crossed Erika's face. She held her arrow steady. But she didn't let it go.

"This fighting has to stop once and for all!" Laura said, her voice growing louder. "It's why our ancestors were banished in the first place! The Lysors say that Hexia was evil."

The Lysors shouted in agreement.

Laura continued, "The Hexors say Lysoria was evil."

The Hexors nodded and grunted.

Laura looked up at the moons in the sky. She felt as though she was seeing them—*really* seeing them—for the very first time. "There was no good twin or evil twin," she said. "They were just sisters who never learned how to share."

As the rot spread to the edges of the tree, Laura spotted one last fresh gray pear dangling from a branch. She leaped up and plucked it. Then she held it out to Erika. "Here."

"It's a trick!" Hugo shouted.

Erika's eyes shifted back and forth as if she were trying to crack a code in her head.

"It's not a trick," said Laura. "It's a gift."

Millie took a step forward. "And it's delicious."

Erika cautiously took the pear. She bit into it with her black teeth. The juice dribbled down her chin. For the very first time, she tasted something fresh. Even though it was just a mushy bland gray pear, her face lit up and her eyes grew wide. "It's . . . good." She took another bite. "It's . . . *really* good." She smacked her lips. "It's . . . the best thing I've ever tasted in my life!" She tossed the gray pear to Hugo. "You've got to try this!"

Hugo took a big bite of the gray pear. As he chewed, he was overwhelmed with joy and confusion all at once. "Why doesn't it taste like death?"

"Because it's not rotten!" said Erika.

"Amazing!" Hugo exclaimed.

The Hexors gathered around Erika and Hugo, eager to try the gray pear for themselves. Laura and Millie smiled at each other. Reina proudly put her hand on Laura's shoulder.

Torian approached Laura, his hands outstretched. "Remarkable," he said, a look of awe on his face. "Laura, you're simply remarkable." He turned to the crowd. "Friends—and I mean everyone here—what we're witnessing today is a historic event. A turning point. With the help of our dear friend, Laura, we can finally do what should have been done long, long ago." He grabbed the crown and ripped it from Laura's hands. "Send the Hexors back to the Putrid Forest and seal it up forever!"

Torian planted the crown firmly on his head.

There was a flash of white light, and the Hexors were thrown violently to the ground.

"No!" Laura cried. "The Hexors deserve to be free!" She lunged at Torian to take the crown off his head, but with another flash of white light, he sent her flying backward. She landed hard in the dirt.

"You sound just like my fool of a sister," Torian said, shaking his head and smiling.

As Laura looked up into his face, she saw that behind his grin was something sinister. Something terrible.

"It was you, wasn't it?" she said, dragging herself to her feet. "You betrayed Queen Ailix. You helped Bloato get into the throne room. You're the reason she's dead!"

Torian's smile curled into a sneer. "It was for your own good!" he barked. "I did what I had to do!"

Shouts of anger reverberated through the crowd of Lysors. They rushed at Torian, crying, "Traitor!" and "Murderer!"

With a flash of the Crystal Crown, the earth shook and a stone tower rose up from beneath Torian, lifting him high into the air, far out of reach from the angry Lysors below.

"Fools! Don't you see?" Torian called down. "When my sister told me she'd freed our mortal enemies, I knew she wasn't fit to wear this crown. It was madness! The Hexors would come for the crown! They would kill us all! Just look at them!" He pointed at the Hexors writhing in pain on the ground. "I *had* to take the crown from my sister so I could keep the Lysors safe. So yes, I made a deal with a goblin—get me the crown, and I'll fill your filthy little cave with more gold and jewels than you could ever imagine. A fair price to pay to put the Hexors back in their cage of rot, no? Bloato was supposed to steal the crown and deliver it to me, not take it for himself. But I should have known—never trust a goblin."

Torian ran his finger along the edge of the crown on his head and smirked. "Still, it all worked out. I'll finally put an end to our war with the Hexors—by winning it! Forget the Putrid Forest—I'll wipe the Hexors off the face of the earth!" He stretched out his arms wide. "My friends, it's time to bow down to me! Bow down to your new king, Torian!"

A long moment of silence hung in the air. Then, one by one, the Lysors did bow their heads. But it wasn't to Torian. It was to Laura.

Torian smirked. "A queen without a crown. What good is that?"

Laura looked up at Torian. "I'm not a queen. I'm an explorer. And you're not a king. You're a liar."

Torian let out a snarl of rage. "All I ever did was try to keep you safe! But I see now that you Lysors aren't worth saving!" He cracked his knuckles. "I'll destroy you all—

Hexors and Lysors—then I'll have all the power and no one will ever take the crown away from me!"

The Crystal Crown flashed with light. From the distance, there was a screeching cry, followed by the crashing sound of enormous footsteps. A creature crested the hills, so vicious and horrible, it looked like it was conjured from a nightmare. It was a giant black rat, as tall as the pine trees, with eyes so red, they could have been pools of blood. Its sharp front teeth dripped black drool that burned the forest floor as it raced toward Hillview.

AS THE GIANT RAT leaped over the ruins of the West Wall, the Lysors and Hexors were paralyzed with fear. Laura and Millie clung to each other, shaking. But then, they heard a sound from behind them—a roaring burp. The strong smell of fish filled their noses.

Millie gasped. "Is that—?"

They looked up and saw Hobbly Knobbly flying over the East Wall, clutching the reins of a Draguin. But this wasn't the puny, waddling Draguin they had seen in the stables. It was a dragon-sized penguin that soared through the air with ease. The kind of Draguin that only the power of the Crystal Crown could have created when they flew over Hobbly Knobbly's house.

"Hee-haw!" Donkeycorn brayed excitedly.

"Now, Draguin!" Hobbly Knobbly shouted, pulling back on the reins. The Draguin opened its beak and sprayed flames onto the ground in front of the rat, stopping it in its tracks.

The rat reared up on its back legs, baring its teeth at the Draguin. And then it charged.

The two creatures collided in a mess of black drool and fire. They crashed to the ground and rolled across the rubble of the fallen walls. As the massive beasts careened toward the Endless Well, the Lysors and Hexors retreated under the Food-Giving Tree.

Torian screwed up his face in anger. There was another flash from the Crystal Crown, and the rat grew larger. Stronger. It pinned down the Draguin, knocking Hobbly Knobbly off. The Draguin squirmed beneath the rat's giant paws.

Hobbly Knobbly staggered over to Laura. "She's running out of strength!" He shuddered. "She can't make it much longer!"

The rat swiped its razor-sharp claws across the Draguin's wing. The Draguin squawked in pain.

"We have to take down Torian!" Laura cried.

"How?" said Millie. "The Crystal Crown is powerful beyond the strongest mind!"

Laura looked at everyone huddled underneath the Food-

Giving Tree, their green and violet locks glowing dimly. "Maybe it's not more powerful than all of our minds working together!"

The Hexors and Lysors glanced at each other with uncertainty.

"Come on," said Erika, taking Laura's hand. "What are you all waiting for?!"

For the very first time since the forging of the Crystal Crown, the Lysors and the Hexors gathered together and joined hands. In between each Lysor was a Hexor, and in between each Hexor was a Lysor. In the crowd, Laura saw Reina, Millie, all of Millie's family right down to baby Georgie, and even blockheaded Claude, standing with the Hexors. They were ready to fight together. Except for poor Quin, who still lay motionless at the base of the Food-Giving Tree. Hobbly Knobbly sat beside him, wiping the sweat from Quin's forehead.

The Draguin kicked at the rat, trying to get free, but the rat sunk its teeth into the Draguin's leg. The Draguin let out a cry of agony and tried to shoot fire out of her beak, but all that came out was a wisp of smoke.

"She needs fire!" Hobbly Knobbly called out.

"Together!" Laura commanded. "Now!"

The Lysors and the Hexors shouted, "Tier'e!"

The Draguin burped out a flame, but it was so tiny, it could barely light a candle.

"It's not enough!" Millie cried.

Just then, Laura heard the hollow sound of heavy rocks rolling as Micah pushed himself out of the rubble of their home.

"Found it!" Micah shouted triumphantly.

He stumbled over to the Food-Giving Tree and knelt down next to Quin. He was holding a glass bottle of pale orange tonic. Laura recognized it. It was the same tonic her dad had refused to take for himself days earlier.

Micah looked to Laura. "Only a few drops left." He dribbled the remaining liquid into Quin's mouth. Quin gasped, and his eyes shot open. His face flushed with color. Laura's heart almost burst with joy.

"It worked!" said Hobbly Knobbly, pulling Quin into a hug.

Laura ran to Quin and grabbed his hand. "We need you now more than ever. You too, Dad."

Quin and Micah joined the others.

"Together!" Laura commanded again.

Torian pounded his fists on the edge of the tower. He shouted at the rat, "What are you waiting for? Kill that oversized penguin!"

The crown flashed. The rat grew to double the size of the Draguin. It opened its massive jaws, about to take the Draguin's head clean off.

All at once, everyone shouted, "Tier'e!"

Even Donkeycorn let out a "Hee-haw!"

So many locks glowed green and violet that it was almost blinding. The Draguin opened its beak, and a blast of flames shot up like a river of fire, knocking the rat onto its back. The rat kicked its feet in the air, squeaking in fear.

"Get up!" Torian bellowed. The Crystal Crown flashed again, but its light was outshone by the locks of glowing hair. Violet and green swirled together into a brilliant amber, just like the color of the fox Laura had seen through the cracks in the wall. All of Hillview was illuminated with a power stronger than the Crystal Crown.

The rat staggered to its feet. No longer controlled by the crown, it fixed its eyes on Torian.

"It looks hungry," Millie whispered.

"For something rotten," said Laura.

The rat ran at Torian, who didn't even have time to scream before it snatched him from the top of the tower in its black fangs. The Crystal Crown fell from Torian's head. Then the rat scurried away, disappearing into the hills, taking Torian with it.

The Lysors and Hexors let go of one another's hands. The Crystal Crown lay in the grass at the base of the tower. No one spoke. No one blinked. Laura could feel all eyes on her. Even the moons in the sky seemed to be looking down at her. She marched over to the crown and picked it up. She had only one use for its mighty power.

"Together, we are more powerful than any crown," she said. For the first time, she placed the Crystal Crown on her head. And with a flash of light, the crown exploded into a trillion pieces that scattered across the entire world. "Whether this is your new home or your old home, Hillview belongs to all of us."

***

The Hexors and the Lysors joyfully set to work rebuilding the town. And Laura was right. Working together, there was no limit to their powers. They brought the Never-Dark trees back to life. As the forest glowed violet and green, it was more dazzling than ever. They cleansed the water in the Clear Lake and refilled the Endless Well. They revived the Food-Giving Tree, and the Hexors' mouths watered at the hundreds of fresh gray pears on the branches. The Hexors helped the Lysors repair their homes, while the Lysors helped the Hexors build new homes using the rubble from Hillview's fallen walls.

Laura found Millie by the Endless Well, her brothers and sisters gathered at her feet.

"So then the troll started shaking the bridge like crazy! I thought we were going to fall to our deaths!" said Millie, gesturing dramatically.

"This is the best bedtime story ever!" said Horton.

Laura wrapped Millie up in a hug.

"You're crushing my lungs!" Millie gasped.

Laura laughed and let go. "I couldn't have done this without you."

Millie smiled. "I told you gray pears were delicious."

"Okay, I admit it. You were right."

Millie looked to her siblings. "Did everyone hear that? I want it on the record!"

They looked around at the busy Hexors and Lysors.

"Everyone's going to be hungry after all this hard work," Millie said. Her eyes grew wide and she clapped her hands together. "I know! I'll make a Thew for everyone! It'll be the biggest Thew you've ever seen in your life!"

Millie's brothers and sisters cheered, and they all ran off to collect as many gray pears as they could find.

Laura and Millie walked to the edge of the Never-Dark Forest, where Micah was wrapping a strand of green hair around the Draguin's wing. Quin and Hobbly Knobbly looked on as the wound began to heal.

"Wow," said Quin.

"Incredible!" said Hobbly Knobbly.

"Hee-haw!" said Donkeycorn, nuzzling the Draguin.

Laura and Millie put their arms around Quin.

"We're so glad you're okay!" Millie exclaimed.

"You risked your life for us. Again!" Laura beamed. "Thank you."

Quin shrugged, blushing a little. "I just wish I could have seen Bloato's face when you snatched the crown off his head."

Laura grinned. "What are you going to do now?"

Quin cast his eyes to the ground. "I guess I'll go home."

"Out of the question!" Hobbly Knobbly bellowed. "You'll

live with me. Just because small mages don't have families doesn't mean we can't make our own. Besides, I need someone to help me take care of the animals. That Crystal Crown made the Centaardvark grow to the size of a house! We're going to have to feed it a *lot* of ants."

Quin smiled wryly. "Have I told you about the nutritional benefits of the beetle butt?"

Reina ran over to Laura and Micah. "Look!" she said, pointing to their house. It was rebuilt. As good as new.

"It's perfect," said Laura.

"The best part about exploring is having a home to come back to," said Reina.

As Laura walked toward her house hand in hand with her mom and dad, she realized that for the first time in her life, the unscratchable itch was gone. She'd had to leave her home in order to save it. But now it was the only place she wanted to be.

FANTASY CREATION ZONE

BY QUINTON JOHNSON

CONTENTS

FANTASY CREATION ZONE SHORTCUTS

THE BEGINNING: THE WORLD

THE MIDDLE: THE QUEST

THE END: THE RETURN

APPENDIX

THE RULES OF THIS WORLD ARE UP TO YOU

Writing a fantasy story means making up an imaginary world where *you* decide on every detail.

You might decide to write about a beautiful world, inhabited by magical beings, where even the trees and rocks are full of secret, wondrous power. Or maybe your style is more dark and creepy, and you want to write about evil forces spreading destruction in a miserable, gloomy land. Then again, you could decide to follow your imagination to some surprising, weird places, and invent a bizarre setting, full of alien creatures unlike anything that has ever been imagined before. You could even do a bit of all those things!

Sometimes fantasy stories take place on distant planets or on planes of existence far from our own. But sometimes the imaginary world is hidden right inside our real world, and if you look down the right street, or into the right house, or through the right closet, you'll catch a glimpse of it looking back at you.

No matter what sort of world you prefer, in a fantasy story *everything* is up to you. Nobody else can tell the writer what color the sky needs to be . . . or whether there is such thing as magic . . . or what kinds of creatures can live there. The writer decides on *all* those things.

In this book, we're going to give you lots of ideas for

how to create a fantasy world all your own and then start writing a story about it. Any kind of story can happen in a fantasy world: comedies, mysteries, love stories—anything you find interesting. If there's a certain kind of story you want to write, *go for it*!

But many stories set in fantasy worlds are **adventure** stories. In an adventure story, you take that world you've made and plop something, or someone, *dangerous* right down into the middle of it. The world, and the people or creatures who live there, are in great peril! A hero needs to appear and go on a dangerous quest to set things in the world right again.

Writing a fantasy adventure story is lots of fun, and lets you take your imagination to some wild places, as you invent magical items, monsters, villains, terrifying dungeons, and all sorts of other wonders and dangers for your hero to confront. Like other stories, it usually has a beginning, middle, and end and goes something like this:

The Beginning: *The World*

> We learn about a fantasy world, meet some of the characters who live there, and find out about a big problem.

The Middle: *The Quest*

> A hero goes on a quest, or adventure, in order to solve the problem.

The End: *The Return*

> The hero completes the quest and solves the problem (or fails to solve it).

In the pages that follow, we're going to give you lots of tips and activities to help you create your own world and send a hero on a big adventure to save it. But the most important thing to remember is that writing a fantasy story is all about getting to do what YOU want. If you want to write something different from what we're suggesting, *do it*! We're just here to give you some ideas. The story you tell is all up to you.

HOW THE FANTASY CREATION ZONE WORKS

In the Fantasy Creation Zone, we'll tell you the basics of how to construct a fantasy world and send a hero on an exciting adventure there. As you read through, you'll see three kinds of entries:

Create a World. These sections will be full of tips for imagining your own fantasy world, and then filling that world with mysterious places, extraordinary creatures, and all the other details that will make it a unique, exciting place for readers to visit.

Quest Log. In the Quest Log, we'll look at how to create

a hero character, and then send that hero on an exciting quest full of villains, obstacles, and danger!

Idea Storm. This is where *you* create an adventure! Each Idea Storm will guide you through the steps of writing your own story set in a fantasy world. If you do every Idea Storm, then by the end, you'll have a complete story!

Besides that, we want you to keep in mind two important things:

First, **your story is not going to start out perfect.** You're going to make mistakes, cross things out, change your mind about what should happen, and make a big mess. If you're doing all that stuff, then you're doing things exactly right. *Nobody's* story looks perfect on their first draft. For example, when they were writing *Quest for the Crystal Crown*, Annabeth and Connor knew they wanted Laura to see an animal through the cracks in the wall in Chapter 1. In the first draft, they made it a yellow bird. Then they realized a bird could fly over the walls of Hillview, so it wouldn't be very exciting to Laura. She probably sees birds all the time! So in the second draft, they changed the animal to an orange fox. That's an animal Laura *definitely* wouldn't see in Hillview.

If you're writing with a pencil and paper, it can also be helpful to **skip lines** when you write. That way, it will be easier to cross things out and add new ideas whenever you need.

pleasantly utterly
One sunny, windless day, Laura was looking through the
a fiery orange fox
cracks in the wall when she spotted ~~a yellow bird~~.

Second, give yourself **PERMISSION TO GET WEIRD.** Every fantasy world is different, and yours doesn't need to look *anything* like one that anyone else has ever thought of before. Sure, many fantasy worlds have elves, and dragons, and magic wands—but these things are all made-up, and all of them started out as somebody's weird idea. Imagine, for example, that you had never heard of a magic wand before, and someone started describing it to you: "It's like a normal stick, except *this* stick has special, imaginary powers! If you touch someone with it, they'll turn into a frog! Or you can shoot a lightning bolt right out of the end of it." For someone who'd never heard of a magic wand before, this idea would sound INCREDIBLY WEIRD. In your fantasy world, you need to give yourself permission to come up with ideas that are just as bizarre and that no one has ever thought of before.

Does that mean you need to keep every single weird idea you come up with in your story? Of course not! If you don't like your idea, you can cross it out, erase it, or delete it. But if you write it down first to see how it sounds, you might just come up with something WEIRD . . . and *awesome.*

See that ? Every time it shows up, that means it's the end of a section. If you got here by flipping forward from page 4, flip back and keep reading!

But come back here soon! The next section is fun: It's all about drawing your own map.

Angie, if you think that I love maps just because I'm a pirate . . . well, you're right. I do love maps. That sounds awesome.

THE BEGINNING: THE WORLD

CREATE A WORLD: STARTING WITH A MAP

An idea for a fantasy world can come from anywhere—even a dream.

When Angie Ortiz was trying to think up ideas for a fantasy setting, she had a dream that she was trapped in a box but could see outside through a small sliver of light. This gave her the idea for Hillview, a small town surrounded by huge walls, where the only way people know what's happening outside the town is by looking through a tiny crack. From that simple beginning, she used her imagination to add more and more details, until eventually she made a whole map of the town.

Here's Angie's map:

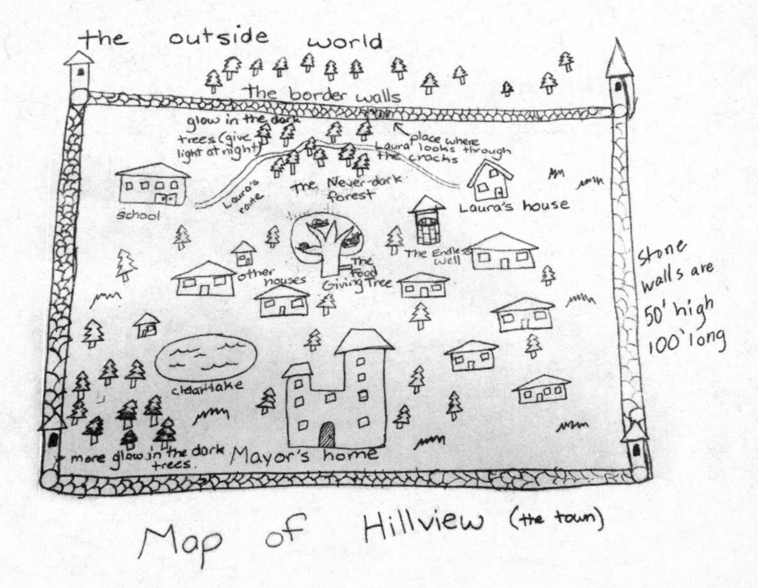

Of course, you don't have to wait for inspiration to come in a dream. Some writers get their first idea from thinking about something really simple: the weather. Maybe they want a land of gigantic deserts, or freezing glaciers, or a very wet world with hundreds of islands, or a world where the sun is blocked out by huge volcanoes erupting constantly—some shooting lava, some shooting ice.

But what if you have no idea where to start? That's okay, too. Sometimes the easiest thing to do is to start with a map and let the ideas come from there. It's easier than it sounds! All you have to do is draw shapes on a piece of paper and see if anything sparks your imagination. For example:

Is the line you're drawing part of a continent? The top of an island? The line of a river? The border of a gigantic desert that stretches out so far nobody has ever been across? Or maybe you don't like the line you're drawing. Just flip the paper over and try again, until you see a shape you like better!

Once you get going, decide what else you want in your

fantasy world. Mountains and trees? Cities and roads? Giant robots and magical fairy waterfalls? You can get as weird as you want. Try coming up with names for everything you're drawing and labeling them on the map. You can use names that you're familiar with (you could name an island after your hometown, or your sister, or one of your pets), or you could make up weird names that nobody has ever heard of before. Just start making nonsense sounds and see what you come up with! ("Garrr . . . bayyyy . . . luuuhhh . . . zoooo . . . Garbailazo Island!") Or you can just name things after the shape it reminds you of: Does that mountain look kind of like a velociraptor head? Make it Raptor Mountain! Did you draw a country that looks sort of like a chair? You could call it Chairland . . . or just use that as a starting place for a made-up name, and change it around until you like the sound of it: "Chairland . . . Charlund . . . Sharlun . . . Lunshar! That's the one!"

Are there big gaps in your map, and you're not sure what to add there? That's great! In fact, that's one of the best things about maps: They tend to be full of blank spaces for your imagination to fill in later when you get a new idea.

Did your map turn out to be a whole gigantic planet or continent? Also great! That will give you a lot of ideas to play with as your story goes on. For the very beginning of your story, however, you'll have an easier time if you choose one town, or city, or small corner of the world, zoom way in, and make a map just of *that* area (like the map of Hillview that Angie drew, on page 184). It will be much easier to start your story with a small area you know a lot about. Save the rest of the map for when your main character goes on a big adventure (because they will—more on that soon).

CREATE A WORLD: WHO IS IN YOUR WORLD?

We humans like to think of ourselves as the smartest animal in the world—the only one that can talk, and think intelligently, and truly understand what's happening around us. And maybe that's true. Maybe we are special, and no other animal is as smart as we are.

On the other hand, maybe all the other animals on Earth *can* talk and think. Maybe they just don't like talking to *us*.

In a fantasy world, it's up to *you* what kinds of creatures can talk, and think, and communicate with each other. Many fantasy worlds have humans in them . . . but those humans aren't the only ones talking. Sometimes the animals can talk with each other, and even with humans (when they want to). Sometimes horrible monsters can talk, especially to taunt people and reveal their horrible plans. And sometimes there are **imaginary people** in the fantasy world who are different from humans in important ways.

As with everything else in your fantasy world, the way these imaginary people work is up to you. Sometimes they might be part human, part animal (maybe they have the bodies and legs of a horse, like centaurs, or maybe they have wings and can fly). Sometimes they are very weird and alien and look nothing like any human, or any animal, on Earth. And sometimes they look a lot like humans but have important differences. They could be bigger, or smaller, or have heads shaped a little differently, or have a third arm, etc. Take the Lysors in *Quest for the Crystal Crown*, for example:

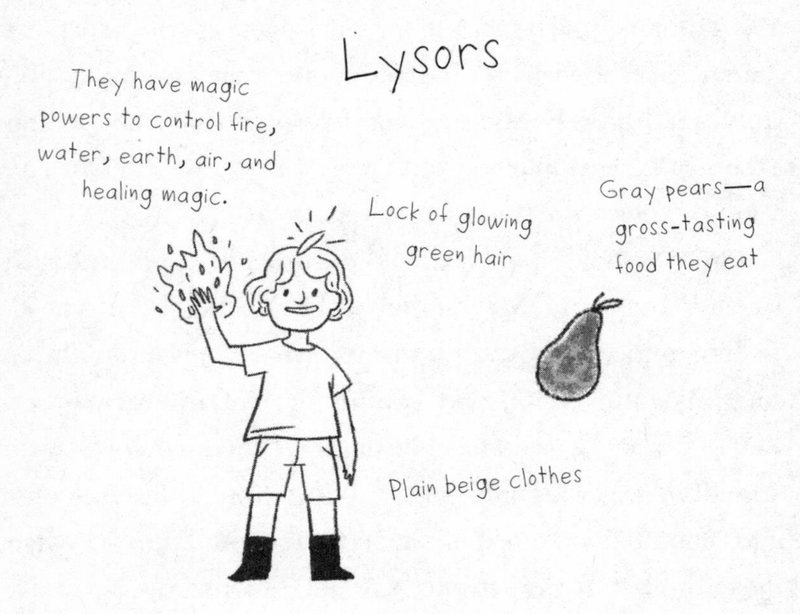

The glowing green hair is weird, but it's such a small detail that if Lysors wanted to disguise themselves as humans, all they'd need to do would be to cover their heads (and in fact, that's exactly what's going to happen in a few chapters). They also have magical powers: They are healers and have some control over the elements of nature. We haven't learned much about this magic yet, but you'll be finding out a lot more as the story goes on.

To help you plan out imaginary people for your world, draw a picture, like we did of the Lysors, and label the most important details you want to remember. This will come in handy when you start to think about your main character (more on that soon). Also, the Lysors aren't the only imaginary people in *Quest for the Crystal Crown*. Keep an eye out, because there are going to be some new, very different people showing up soon. . . .

QUEST LOG: WELCOME TO THE WORLD

So let's say you have a map, and you've imagined lots of details about your fantasy world, including what sort of people live there. How do you actually start *writing* a fantasy story?

The short version is: You should show your readers around your imaginary world! After all, you spent some time making it up, so you probably think it's cool! But at the same time, you want to make sure you're showing it to them in an interesting way that will get their attention.

One simple way to start is to write about what people are *doing* in your world on a regular day. You should especially think about what they're doing that is *weird* or *unexpected* or *exciting*, and that will tell the reader something about the world you've created. Are there huge walls in your setting, and nobody can get in or out? You might begin by writing about someone desperately trying to look through the cracks. Or is your world incredibly cold and covered in ice? You could start off your story by showing some people going about their daily business on the giant super glacier. ("Let's ice-skate a couple of miles over to the grocery store—it's not as cold as usual, you'll only need to wear three coats.") Or maybe your world has really weak gravity, and kids play a sport where they try to jump over the roofs of the houses in their neighborhood. ("Watch out for the chimney!") Whatever your world is like, decide what weird or interesting things people there are *doing*, and you'll have an interesting place to start writing.

And here's a bonus idea: To help the reader understand *exactly* what it's like in your world, choose *exactly* the right words to describe it. As you start off your story, you want your readers to feel like they're right there in the middle of things. They should feel the rocks under your characters' feet, or the cold breeze blowing through their hair, or the fear as they look out into a dark, foggy swamp, unsure what's in front of them as they take step after soggy step through the mud. . . .

To help do that, we have a list of words you can use to describe different kinds of settings. Is your world cold? Don't just tell the reader that it's "cold" over and over again! Look at our list, and shake things up by telling your reader about the "frigid" temperatures. Or don't just say it's "hot"—let the reader know about the "scorching" heat of the sun. You get the idea! Check out our list:

WORDS FOR PLACES THAT ARE . . .

Empty, with few plants or animals	Full of plants and animals	Unbelievably stinky
barren	abundant	fetid
desolate	bountiful	putrid
forsaken	lush	rancid
uninhabited	verdant	reeking

Scary	Rocky
direful	bouldered (full of big rocks)
eerie	gravelly (full of small rocks)
ghoulish	jagged (full of sharp rocks)
ominous	rugged (lots of climbing up and down)

These words aren't only for the beginning of a story, either! Keep coming back here anytime you want to find exactly the right word to describe part of your world.

IDEA STORM: WRITE YOUR WORLD

Now you try it! Write the very beginning of a story, where you let the reader know about your imaginary world.

You can start by brainstorming *tons* of details about that world. You might draw a map to help you get ideas (see page 184), or draw pictures of the imaginary people you'd like to live there (see page 187). Come up with as many details as you can, and remember that you always have PERMISSION TO GET WEIRD! Do your best to create a world unlike anything that's been written about before.

Once you have some ideas, you can start your story. One interesting way to begin is to write about something weird or unusual that the people in your world are *doing*. Are they magically growing food? Dodging volcanic eruptions? Playing a weird sport that nobody has ever heard of before? There's no wrong answer to what they might be doing. The only thing that's important is choosing an activity that makes sense for *your* world—maybe even an activity that would *only* happen in the weird, unique world you've imagined.

Where does your story go from there? Keep reading! We've got more ideas coming right up.

QUEST LOG: THE HERO

You might not be able to tell quite yet, but Laura isn't just any main character: She's going to be a **hero.** The moment she saw that arrow flying through the air was just the beginning of what will turn into a big adventure.

The difference between a normal main character and a **hero** is the size of the problem they're going to be facing. A heroic character needs a HUGE, Hero-Sized Problem. We'll see some examples of Hero-Sized Problems after the next chapter, but in short: It's a problem where *lots* of people (a whole community, or city, or country, or entire fantasy world) need a hero to save them from danger. A hero doesn't deal with problems that affect only *themselves;* they need to *save people.* (Laura doesn't know this yet, but the whole town of Hillview is about to be in big trouble. Keep reading. . . .)

Heroes can come in all shapes and sizes.

Some are the strongest and most powerful people in the land. They might be brimming with ancient magic, giving off a glow as they bend the forces of time and space to turn their enemies into harmless kittens with a sweep of their hands. Or they might swing a huge sword, their armor flashing in the sun as they charge toward a terrifying dragon. Or perhaps they fly through the air, not bothered by heat or cold, diving down into smoldering volcanoes and icy seas to save innocent people crying out for help.

On the other hand, some heroes are more unexpected. Like Laura, they might look like a regular kid going about their day—nobody would ever suspect that the courageous heart of a hero beats inside them and that they will never, ever give up until the job is done. Or for some heroes, the extraordinary thing about them is their mind: They're not the strongest or the fastest, and they don't know magic, but they can outsmart much stronger enemies with cunning, creative plans. Then again, some heroes are simply born leaders who know how to get lots of people to follow them: They give awesome speeches to rally people to help those in need or inspire others with their bravery and compassion. A hero is much stronger if surrounded by lots of friends and admirers.

Or maybe you want to write about a hero that is just plain weird! Some heroes have very unexpected talents and powers and make the reader laugh with the bizarre ways they find to solve problems and help people. For more on this kind of hero, check out the next section on page 202: "Hero's Talent Challenge."

The most important thing is to create a hero that YOU are excited about. You can choose *any* of the kinds of heroes we just listed . . . or you could write about *several* of these kinds of heroes, working together to accomplish a quest . . . or even *none* of these kinds of heroes—maybe you have a totally different idea you want to try. That's great! The only thing that really matters is finding a character who is going to solve a HUGE problem and help lots of people.

On page 201, we filled out a Hero Creator, which is designed to help you come up with interesting details about your own hero. Our version shows Laura so you can see how it works. Let's look at each of the prompts on the Hero Creator, one at a time:

Draw your hero! Label important details you want to remember. Drawing can be a great way to come up with ideas. As you can see here, Laura is a regular girl . . . except she has the glowing green hair of a Lysor and longs to find adventure outside the walls of her small village.

Hero's name. In your fantasy world, it's up to you how names should work. They can be normal-sounding names from our own world (like Laura, Millie, etc.). They can be weirder-sounding names, from your imagination (these could really be anything: Merpo, Pthhpop, whatever you can think up). Or you can decide that in your world, names work in a totally different way. For example, maybe everyone in your world says their parents' names and something about their town when they introduce themselves: "I am Rarlage, son of Duggie and Rulah, of the great boat-making city of South Ferry." Or maybe they get their names in an unusual way: "When I was a baby, before I could talk, I used to make the sound *'Bah-boo.'* That is why my name is Bah-boo."

What is your hero really good at, or what is your hero's talent? What **talents** make your hero a force to be reckoned with? Are they incredibly strong? Good at magic? Sneaky?

Courageous? Or is it something more unusual? In Laura's case, her talent is her love of adventure: She is just really, *really* curious about the outside world. She wants to see as much of the world as she can, and this drives her to take risks and be brave in situations when other people would be too terrified to do anything. If you want more ideas for heroes with unusual talents, check out the Hero's Talent Challenge on page 202!

What is your hero NOT good at, or what are they afraid of? Every hero has some kind of **weakness**—if they didn't, then the story wouldn't be very interesting! They'd just solve the problem instantly and never be in any danger. Picking a big, interesting weakness for your hero—and then putting them in situations where they'll have to deal with that weakness—is important for keeping things exciting. Laura has a few weaknesses: For one thing, she is very independent and doesn't work well on a team—which is going to cause her problems if she ever has to work together with others. But her biggest weakness is that she's a kid going on a big, adult adventure! She's not super strong, or super magical, or super experienced at doing heroic things. She'll probably meet people, animals, and monsters who are much stronger and more powerful than she is, and she's going to be in danger a lot (which is going to make the story very exciting!)

What is your hero's biggest dream in life? We all have dreams we hope to accomplish—and so do heroes! Any dream will work for your hero, and for you as a writer, this can be a key to making your character *do* interesting things over the course of the story. Laura dreams of being an explorer just like her mom—which is going to make her very excited to explore, as soon as she has a chance (which she will, very soon). Does your hero dream of having a cool pet? Maybe every time they see an animal on their adventure, they'll try to make friends with it. Do they dream of eating the tastiest ice cream of all time? Maybe they're always trying to collect interesting ingredients for an ice cream recipe. Do they dream of becoming a star basketball player? Maybe they're always trying to find ways to practice making shots, even if there are no basketballs around, so they practice by throwing rocks into the mouth of a dragon. You get the idea!

Who is your hero's helper? Most heroes can't do their job alone. They're going to need some help along the way. When Laura wanted to look out over the wall, it was Millie who helped her—and Millie is going to continue to be important for Laura as the story goes on. Even heroes need someone they can trust and to support them when the going gets tough. There are different kinds of helpers your hero might have:

- *The sidekick.* This is a character who goes on an adventure with the hero and helps throughout the whole story. The hero is in charge, but the sidekick is always nearby when the hero needs an extra boost (like Millie is for Laura). You might also choose to have the sidekick be good at things the hero is NOT good at, to make them the best team possible. For example, if the hero is very smart and sneaky but not all that strong, the sidekick might have incredible strength to help out in those situations where they'll need to lift a giant boulder, or wrestle a huge alligator monster, etc.

- *The teacher.* Whatever the hero's talent is, the teacher has been helping them to better use their skills. Later on in the adventure, when the hero is climbing a mountain . . . or driving a flying car . . . or using magic . . . or dodging attacks from stone statues who have come to life . . . the hero will think back on advice this teacher gave them and use it to accomplish a goal. ("Remember what your teacher always said: Stone statue monsters are strong, but they're *slow.* Focus on dodging.") The teacher may also offer important advice about the dangers the hero will face on the adventure. ("If a tree in the swamp offers you a slice of cake, whatever you do, DON'T EAT IT.") Or they may even recount a riddle or prophecy that the hero will have to decipher later. ("It is said that when the three planets form a triangle atop the pyramid, in that moment the door will be revealed.")

- *The motivator.* Sometimes, in the beginning of a story, the hero doesn't want to go on an adventure or solve a big problem. Maybe they're scared, or don't believe they have the skills, or just think that it's not their responsibility—someone else should be the hero! In that case, your hero may need a motivator: a helper who convinces them to step up and be a hero. The motivator might give them extra courage. ("I believe in you! With your talents I know you'll succeed!") Or they might try to convince them logically. ("If you don't do this, who else will? Someone needs to take up the challenge.") Or they might even get angry with them. ("You sicken me! Don't be a coward!") It doesn't matter who this motivator is. They could be a parent, a friend, a next-door neighbor, a magical talking dog—all that matters is that they pump up the hero to deal with a big, scary problem.

HERO CREATOR

Draw your hero! Label important details you want to remember.

Hero's name: Laura

What is your hero really good at, or what is your hero's talent?

She loves adventure, and she's not afraid to explore the unknown.

What is your hero NOT good at, or what are they afraid of?

She's just a regular kid! She's not super strong or super powerful. It will be dangerous for her to be a hero.

What is your hero's biggest dream in life?

To become an explorer like her mother.

Who is your hero's helper?

Millie: Laura's cousin and best friend. She doesn't love adventure and gets scared easily, but she wants to help Laura.

As you create your hero, think about what kinds of helpers might join them on their adventure, or teach them important skills, or even just convince them to step up and be a hero in the first place! There can also be more than one helper. We focused on Millie here, but Laura will definitely be finding more help along the way in this story.

QUEST LOG: HERO'S TALENT CHALLENGE

Are you tired of watching the same old heroes on TV every day? Have you read about so many heroes with the same superpowers that you think, "I wish they would do something *new* and *different*"? Do you see heroes shooting magic lasers at each other and think, "Can't you *surprise* me for once, and change the rules of the hero game?"

If you're having thoughts like those, then you've come to the right place! Welcome to the Hero's Talent Challenge.

In this challenge, we're going to help you flip the script and *surprise* your readers with heroes totally unlike what they're used to. The place to start is with the hero's **talents.** Every hero has talents, or powers, or things they're good at, but we're going to help you practice coming up with *weird*, unusual talents. Talents that you might think have nothing at all to do with saving people and solving big problems. And most of the time, you'd be right: Usually heroes don't have talents like these—which is what makes this a challenge! But it's also what will make these heroes new and interesting.

Here's how it works: Take a look at the following list of Unusual Hero Talents. Choose one, or make up your own. (Maybe this list will give you an idea for a different, very unusual talent.)

UNUSUAL HERO TALENTS

Singing
Dancing
Cooking
Swimming
Whistling
Doing magic tricks (not real magic—just tricks)
Playing an instrument
Training animals
Writing stories
Knitting sweaters
Being a door-to-door salesperson
Spinning a basketball on one finger
Telling jokes
Making sandwiches
Sneezing
Jumping rope
Balancing on one leg
Having shiny hair
Making funny sound effects
Being very fluffy and cute

Next, you're going to choose an **obstacle.** Don't worry—this isn't a big, Hero-Sized Problem yet. It's just a Warm-Up Obstacle. Consider it a training mission for your hero, where they face a smaller problem and see if they can figure out a way to get past it. Go ahead and choose one (or make up your own Warm-Up Obstacle, if these give you an idea):

WARM-UP OBSTACLES

- There's a canyon, forty feet wide, blocking the hero's path.
- A herd of angry cats is attacking the hero.
- A pack of cute dogs is trying to lick the hero.
- A monkey stole the hero's food.
- The road is incredibly icy and hard to walk on.
- The hero steps in quicksand.
- Garbage is flying in through the windows of the hero's house.
- A boat carrying the hero is sinking.
- A boat carrying the hero is on fire.
- A boat carrying the hero comes to life and won't let anyone steer it.
- Ducks are pecking the hero's feet.
- The hero's hand got glued to the side of a stone wall—the hero's stuck!
- The hero is lost inside a dark cave.
- The hero is stuck high up on a tall tower with no way down.
- The hero needs to get over a one-hundred-foot-high wall.

- The wind is blowing so hard that the hero starts to fly away.
- It's raining so hard that the hero starts to float away.
- It's snowing so hard that the hero is getting buried underneath the snow.
- A wizard turned the roof of the hero's house into a pancake, and birds are eating through it.
- A giant guitar is so loud it's causing musical earthquakes.

Now comes the fun part! Try to figure out how the hero could use their Unusual Hero Talent to get past the Warm-Up Obstacle. This will be most interesting if you pick a talent that seems like it has *nothing to do* with the obstacle. For example, let's say you chose "Having shiny hair" for your talent and "The hero steps in quicksand" for your obstacle. You might ask: "What does having shiny hair have to do with quicksand?" It's not an easy question, but that's why you have PERMISSION TO GET WEIRD! There's not a wrong answer.

Maybe when they get stuck in quicksand, the hero points their shiny hair toward a nearby town to signal for help. Maybe birds are fascinated by the shiny hair, so the hero calls some over—then the birds grab on to the hair and pull the hero up. Or maybe the hair is so shiny it reflects the heat of the sun onto the quicksand and evaporates all the water to turn it into regular sand.

You can probably come up with other answers, too! In a fantasy story, the rules of how the talent works are up to you. Try stretching your imagination with this challenge—or try stumping your family and friends to see who can come up with the best way for a hero with an unexpected talent to get past an obstacle.

IDEA STORM: INTRODUCING THE HERO

Now make up your own hero! Draw your own version of the Hero Creator on page 201, and use it to come up with ideas for a hero character that fits *your* fantasy world. Will they be human, or some kind of imaginary person? Will they be extremely strong and powerful, or will they be someone you'd never expect to be a hero at first glance? Remember that a hero can be *anybody*, as long as they'll rise to the challenge of solving a HUGE problem and saving people.

What will your hero's talents be? If you want to create a new and unusual hero, practice by choosing an Unusual Hero Talent and a Warm-Up Obstacle from the Hero's Talent Challenge on page 202. Be sure to also decide on something they're NOT good at, and give them a helper of some kind. The helper doesn't have to be a sidekick that sticks with them for the whole story (though they can be) but can be anybody who gives the hero advice, or training, or even just motivates them to get out there and be a hero!

Once you have a hero character, start writing about them! One place you could begin is by giving the hero a Warm-Up Obstacle and describing how they get past it. This will let the reader see a glimpse of the hero in action so they have an idea of what the hero will be like when real danger strikes later in the story. You could also introduce the hero by showing the reader something about their greatest dream in life: If they want to be a basketball player, write about them playing basketball! If they want to eat the most delicious ice cream ever, write about them taste-testing ice cream! If they want to be an explorer, write about them trying to see over a giant wall and catching sight of danger. . . .

QUEST LOG: HERO-SIZED PROBLEMS AND THE VILLAINS WHO CAUSE THEM

Let's get this out of the way first: You don't *need* a villain character in your fantasy world. You can write an incredible adventure story where the big problem doesn't come from a villain at all, especially if you create an interesting "Hero-Sized Problem."

Any character in any story can have a problem, big or small. ("Oh no! I stepped in a puddle! Now my shoes are wet!") A Hero-Sized Problem, on the other hand, is a problem SO big that it affects an entire community. ("Oh no! The puddle has mysteriously grown, and now it's spread over the entire town! *Everyone* is wet, and the water is still rising!") Only a hero can find a way to solve this problem!

There are lots of different ways to come up with a Hero-Sized Problem. For starters, you could do exactly what we did in the last paragraph: Think of a very small problem ("A squirrel just bit my toe!") and decide how you could make that small problem grow, and grow, until you have a HUGE, Hero-Sized Problem on your hands ("Angry squirrels have overrun the city! They're attacking everyone!").

Another way to come up with a Hero-Sized Problem is to imagine a huge natural disaster: a meteor speeding toward the planet, or a gigantic volcanic eruption, or a powerful storm. You could also imagine a much weirder and more imaginary disaster: Maybe that meteor is actually a terrible space monster, or maybe the lava shooting into the town isn't coming from a volcano but from the chimney of a tiny cottage in the woods, or maybe that powerful storm lasts for years and years and forces a whole kingdom to flee somewhere safer. . . . Or maybe there is a problem with your world that is SO weird it's never been thought of before until it enters your imagination.

Any of those Hero-Sized Problems could happen without a villain being involved at all. If you don't want a villain in your story, all you need is to create a HUGE problem that affects a whole community, and then decide what the hero needs to do to save everyone.

But on the other hand . . . writing about villains is fun! So is reading about them. If it wasn't, there wouldn't be so many stories about them. If you're planning out an adventure story of your own, chances are you'll *want* to create a villain who's causing the Hero-Sized Problem. Let's take a look at some of the most popular kinds of villains so you can decide which one might be right for you:

- *The villain who wants to take over.* Some villains just want to be in charge. Their biggest dream is to take over and boss everyone around. This is a very popular choice for fantasy adventure stories, but it's been done so many times that for a writer, it's actually a challenge to make this kind of villain exciting. You'll need to find ways to make your villain's plan new and interesting so that your readers don't get bored with *yet another* story about a villain trying to take over the town. For tips on how to do exactly that, read "So You Want to Take Over the Town . . ." on page 217!

FANTASY CREATION ZONE

- *The villain who wants to destroy.* This villain is similar to the one who wants to take over, except they are interested only in destruction. They don't want to take something over, they just want to bury it under lava, or sweep it away with a powerful wind, or magically make it disappear. This is probably the hardest kind of villain to do well, because to make this villain interesting—or to make this villain even *make sense* at all—you have to think very, very hard about *why* they would want to be so destructive. *Why* would they want to blow up the world with a magic fireball? What are they going to do after that's done, besides just sit around on a smoldering, burned-up fire-world eating popcorn all alone? What's the point? We're not saying it's impossible to write about this kind of villain, we're just saying it's hard to make them make sense. Think very carefully before picking this one.
- *The villain with a BIG project.* This villain is working on something BIG! They've got an incredible idea for a new invention . . . or new kind of magic . . . or new kind of travel . . . or new kinds of creatures they want to bring to life, etc. The only problem is, there are also BIG side effects! This new invention has the power to hurt people . . . or this new kind of magic freezes farmers' crops . . .

or this new kind of travel rips a hole in the universe . . . or these new kinds of creatures are dangerous and frightening, etc. The villain thinks that their BIG project is so important these side effects don't matter, even if people get hurt. But the hero disagrees.

- *The hidden villain.* At first, it seems like there isn't actually a villain. Maybe there's a natural disaster, like a volcano, or a more mysterious disaster, like monsters appearing in the woods. At first, the hero is concerned only with helping people through this disaster . . . but then, it turns out a villain is secretly behind the whole thing. *Why* is the villain causing a volcano to go off, or causing monsters to appear, or causing whatever else the problem is? That part is up to you: Maybe it's the first step in a plan to take over the town . . . maybe it's a side effect from a BIG project they're working on . . . or maybe it's something much weirder! In any case, it can be fun to have the villain be hidden at first, and then surprise the reader.
- *The legendary villain.* This is very similar to the hidden villain, except you give the audience hints that there *might* be a villain. Nobody knows for *sure* why that volcano is erupting or those monsters are appearing . . . but there are rumors that it's being caused by a hidden villain. Maybe an old man in

town remembers a problem from long ago that was eerily similar, caused by a villain who everyone thought had been banished from the world. Or maybe there is an ancient legend, or prophecy, that a villain would come and cause problems just like the ones happening right now. Or maybe someone who works for the villain is purposefully spreading rumors that a very powerful villain is causing the problem, to scare people, or even to try to get some people to come to the villain's side. The hero will need to investigate and figure out exactly who they're up against. For a writer, this is also a great way to get the audience excited to meet this villain, building up the suspense and mystery, until the villain finally appears later in the story.

- *The personal villain.* In some stories, the villain isn't even behind the Hero-Sized Problem—they're just trying to stop the hero from solving it. For example, maybe they didn't cause the natural disaster, but it fits in with some sort of Villainous Plan. ("I'm the best carpenter in town—if the volcano destroys everyone's homes, they'll have to pay ME to build new ones!") Or maybe they just don't get along with the hero and would enjoy seeing them fail. ("That hero is so annoying—if I stop them from solving the problem, everyone will see the hero isn't as perfect as they think.") Or maybe the villain isn't even such a bad person! Maybe they're just in some sort of competition against the hero. ("If I finish the quest before the hero, I'll be the one to solve the problem! The hero is too weak, anyway—I'm the only one powerful enough to save the town!") Sometimes it's more interesting if the reader can sympathize with the villain and see their point of view.

On page 216, we put together a Hero-Sized Problem organizer to help you come up with ideas for your own Hero-Sized Problem. In our version, we laid out all the details of the problem in *Quest for the Crystal Crown.* Let's take a look at each question to see how it works:

- *What is the Hero-Sized Problem?* There are lots of different Hero-Sized Problems you could put in a story, as we discussed at the beginning of this section. In our case, the town of Hillview is in danger! The Hexors are threatening to come back and destroy it while they look for something called "The Crystal Crown."
- *What SOUND does the problem make?* THWUNK! BOOM! Sometimes people first find out about a Hero-Sized Problem by hearing a strange and terrifying sound. It can be exciting for readers if you write the sound *before* you write anything

about the problem—this will leave them wondering "What was that sound?" There is no one rule for creating a sound word. All you need to do is ask yourself, "How would *my* problem sound?" For example, is a volcano erupting more of a WHOOOOOSH or a KRKRKRKRRRPPKKRR? The sound—and the spelling—is up to you!

- *Is there a villain causing this problem? Who are they?* Drawing and labeling a picture is a great way to brainstorm ideas about a character, so the Hero-Sized Problem organizer includes a picture of Erika and Hugo! We've also let you know that these two aren't the only villains in the story: There's a hidden villain you haven't read about yet. If you're planning a hidden villain for *your* story, you can definitely still draw them and label as many details as you want—but we didn't want to give the hidden villain away just yet, so we left it a mystery for now. (And if you *don't* want a villain in your story, you don't have to answer this question, or either of the ones after it!)
- *Why are they causing this problem?* This is a very important question for a villain—and "because they're evil" isn't going to be a very interesting answer. If the villain *wants* something, and is causing the problem as part of a plan to get what they *want*, your story will be much more interesting.

As we know, Erika and Hugo want the Crystal Crown—and they also blame the Lysors for making them live in the Putrid Forest, so they're out for revenge.

- *How are they doing it?* For Erika and Hugo, this answer is pretty simple: They searched for Hillview for years, and then finally found it. Now they're coming back with an army. For more tips on how to come up with an interesting answer to this question, check out "So You Want to Take Over the Town . . ." on page 217.

FANTASY CREATION ZONE

HERO-SIZED PROBLEM

What is the Hero-Sized Problem? Write or draw details!

The town of Hillview is under attack! The Hexors want to find the "Crystal Crown" and will destroy the town to try to find it. All the Lysors are in danger!

The Hexors broke the north wall!

What SOUND does the problem make?

THWUNK! BOOM!

Is there a villain causing the problem? Who are they? Draw them, and label important details you want to remember.

Erika and Hugo—two Hexors

Spoiler: There is also a hidden villain in this story. We don't want to give it away here, but keep reading. . . .

Why are they causing this problem?

To get the Crystal Crown and take over Hillview. They are angry with the Lysors for trapping them in the Putrid Forest many years ago.

How are they causing this problem?

They searched for Hillview for years. Now that they've found it, they're going to come back with the whole Hexor army.

QUEST LOG: SO YOU WANT TO TAKE OVER THE TOWN . . .

We've all been there.

You're an aspiring villain, and you want to take over the whole town . . . or the whole city . . . or the whole country . . . or even the whole WORLD. It sounds great at first! You'd get to boss everyone around! You'd be super, super rich! You could make people put up statues of you and hang pictures of your face on every wall for all to adore! What's not to love?

But then your plans run into reality. *Every* villain wants to take over the town (. . . or the city . . . or the country . . . or the WORLD). It's been done too many times. People barely even pay attention to your villainous schemes because they've *heard it all before*. Your plans can't get off the ground because the townspeople you're trying to scare can't stop yawning in boredom.

That's why you need the Villainous Plan Generator! It's our new system for aspiring villains, to help you come up with a bold, exciting, creative plan to take over the town that nobody has ever thought of before! It's easy to use and costs you nothing except a pencil and paper to make your plan on.

Let's start with a test drive. Before you make up your own plan, choose one of the sample FIRST STEPS from the following list. Pick whichever one you want, and we'll show you how easy it is to design your own Villainous Plan.

MY FIRST STEP TO TAKE OVER THE TOWN WILL BE . . .

- Start a laundry business, washing everyone's clothes in a magic river.
- Round up all the giraffes and hide them in a cave.
- In the middle of the night, break the main bridge into town so no one can get over it.
- Put a spell on the bakery, causing all the bread to dissolve into sand when anyone tries to eat it.
- Dig a mine deep under the ground.
- Sneak an enchanted book out of the library.
- Sneak an enchanted book *into* the library.
- Cut down all the trees in the very center of the forest.
- Freeze a waterfall solid.
- Learn to speak the language of rats.
- Create magical creatures that look exactly like pancakes.
- Invent a strange new flying machine.
- Buy the biggest farm in the whole kingdom.
- Build an underwater house deep in the ocean.
- Transform into a goose.
- Get extremely good at playing a musical instrument.
- Start a mountain-climbing school.
- Construct a railroad.
- Become a famous firefighter.
- Give away a huge mansion as a present.

When you've chosen one, plug it into the Villainous Plan Generator on page 221. You have PERMISSION to get very WEIRD here as you answer the questions. For example:

- *What is the first step in your Villainous Plan?* Let's say you chose "Round up all the giraffes and hide them in a cave." That's a weird one. How is that going to turn into a Villainous Plan to take over the town?
- *Because of this . . . (How does the first step help you get what you want?)* Well, let's see . . . what do I know about giraffes? They're tall, they eat leaves . . . Maybe this should be: "The trees around town will grow much bigger, with a much thicker covering of leaves, because there are no giraffes to eat the leaves off the top."
- *What is the next step in your Villainous Plan?* Okay . . . how could I use big trees to help me take over a town? What about . . . "I'll use my tree-enchanting spell, and soon these extra big and strong trees will be working for ***me***!"
- *Finally . . . (How do these steps help you get what you want?)* One final step! How could those enchanted trees help me finish off my plan? "The trees won't let anybody in or out of town unless I say so. I'll force the people to put me in charge of the town, or

else I'll hold them all prisoner and not let any food get through from outside. HAHAHAHAHA!"

And sure, maybe a hero will decide to go on a quest to find the giraffes and bring them back to eat the trees down to a normal size . . . but you're a powerful villain! Surely you can stop a puny hero with a plan like that.

Want to keep practicing? Make up your own weird, creative "first steps," or challenge your friends and family to see who can come up with the best ones! When you're ready, you can use the Villainous Plan Generator to create a brand-new Villainous Plan for your story. If four boxes isn't enough, you can also add *more* steps to your own plan. Keep adding as many boxes as you need to see the plan through!

VILLAINOUS PLAN GENERATOR

CAUTION: Villainous Plans are to be used only by villains in fantasy stories. The makers of the Villainous Plan Generator do not endorse or recommend using these plans to actually take over a town.

What is the first step in your Villainous Plan?

I will round up all the giraffes and hide them in a cave!

Because of this . . . (How does the first step help you get what you want?)

The trees around town will grow much bigger, with a much thicker covering of leaves, because there are no giraffes to eat the leaves

What is the next step in your Villainous Plan?

I'll use my tree-enchanting spell, and soon those extra big and strong trees will be working for me!

Finally (How do these steps help you get what you want?)

The trees won't let anybody in or out of town unless I say so. I'll force the people to put me in charge of the town, or else I'll hold them all prisoner, and not let any food get through from outside. HAHAHAHAHAHAHAHAHA!!

IDEA STORM: THE HERO-SIZED PROBLEM

Now write about the Hero-Sized Problem in *your* story!

Be sure to make your problem so HUGE that lots of people are in danger and will need a hero to save them. Maybe you start by imagining a small problem ("There's ice on the road!") and make it bigger and bigger ("There's ice covering the whole town!"), or maybe you come up with a natural disaster ("The volcano is erupting!"), or maybe it's something much weirder ("The castle just vanished! There's a shimmering field of energy where it was standing!").

If there is a villain involved, think up lots of details about what they're like. If you want, you can make them mean and destructive (like the Hexors), but they don't need to be. Just like a hero, a villain can be anybody, as long as they're causing a Hero-Sized Problem . . . or trying to stop a hero from solving a Hero-Sized Problem. You can also use our Villainous Plan Generator on page 221: Make up the villain's "first step," and then work out the rest of the plan from there.

When you actually start writing about the problem, sometimes writing the *sound* the problem makes is an exciting way to begin. One minute, you're telling your reader about a normal day in your world, with the people there tasting ice cream, or playing basketball, or looking over a wall, and then the next minute . . . *thwunk!* What was that?!

Your reader will be excited to keep turning the pages to find out!

QUEST LOG: CHOOSE A QUEST

Bloato wears the Crystal Crown.

What does this mysterious sentence mean? Who is Bloato . . . and where would Laura be able to find him . . . and the crown?

What we've got here, folks, is a **quest.** A quest is *how the hero gets what they need* to solve the Hero-Sized Problem—and usually it involves going on a dangerous adventure, where they're trying to find something very important. Here are some examples:

- *The quest for an object.* Sometimes the hero needs to find a special object to help their community. It may be an object with magical powers (like the Crystal Crown that Laura is after), or some sort of medicine to heal people, or a tool that the hero will need to solve the problem. It may even be an object full of such evil power that *destroying* it will solve the problem.

- *The quest for a person.* The hero might be on a quest to find a person. This could be someone who is in danger, and needs a hero to save them. Or it might be a wise person, who can give the hero important information or special training. Or the person might even be a villain who the hero needs to defeat . . . if they can only catch them first.
- *The quest for a place.* Maybe there's a community in danger, but to reach it, the hero will need to travel far. Or maybe there is a legendary land the hero is looking for, where they believe great wisdom or power can be found. Some heroes even go on a quest to get back to their *own* home—and solve whatever problems await them when they finally arrive.
- *The quest for knowledge.* There may be a forgotten magic spell . . . or a treasure map . . . or an ancient secret about the world, which explains why things are happening in the present day. The hero needs to find this piece of knowledge in order to solve the Hero-Sized Problem.

What all these quests have in common is that they are **very** hard to accomplish. Usually the hero needs to go on a long journey, full of extreme danger and many obstacles, in order to achieve their goal. The quest should be so hard to accomplish, in fact, that it takes an *entire story* for the hero to finally do it.

To help you come up with ideas for your quest, you might also choose to draw and label the **quest object:** the thing, or person, or place the hero is trying to find. Here's our picture of the Crystal Crown.

And once you've decided on a quest . . . congratulations! You're almost done with the **beginning** of your story! Hold on tight, because in the **middle,** the action is going to kick up a notch.

CREATE A WORLD: DIALOGUE

A voice below said, "Where do you think you're going?"

One of the best ways to put the reader into your world, feeling like they're right in the center of the action, is by writing interesting **dialogue** between characters. Hearing characters talk will bring those characters—and the fantasy world—to life like nothing else.

How do you write good dialogue for a fantasy story? There's no magic formula, but here are a few simple tips to get you started:

- *Decide what's special about the way people talk in your world.* Dialogue is a *great* way to show how your fantasy world is different from the real world. For example, you might think about what people in your world say when they meet each other. Do they just say "hello," or do they phrase it very differently? Do they have a weird, unexpected greeting ("Your nose is shiny today, my friend")? Or do they have a greeting that tells us something about their world? For example, do they live in a city on the back of a gigantic insect, and say "Bless the six legs that carry us" whenever they meet? You can also decide how people in your world say good-bye, what they call mealtimes, what they call their parents or children, what their money is called, their names for different jobs (Do they say "doctor" or "healer" or "bandage lady"?), etc. So far in *Quest for the Crystal Crown*, we've seen one big example of people talking in an unusual way, when the Lysors use words from an ancient language (such as *talamh'e*) to cast magic spells. Is *talamh'e* a real word? Nope! The authors just made it up. In *your* world, you are free to make up as many imaginary words as you want—just make sure the reader can figure out what they mean. (For more on magic words, check out "Create a World: Magic" on page 233.)

- *Remember the character.* Writing dialogue can be extra fun if you're writing about heroes and villains. You will get lots of chances for the villain to say something villainous (*"Just go, you drooling oaf!"*) and the heroes to give a heroic speech (*"Everyone deserves to be healed. Lysor or Hexor, it doesn't matter. Always remember that."*). But it's also fun to write dialogue no matter who your characters are! If your character is a goofball, have them say something goofy. (*"I accidentally bit off my whole fingernail."*) If your character is scared of everything, have them say something cowardly. (*"We have to run! We have to hide!"*) Whatever your characters are like, dialogue is a fun way to show off their personalities to the reader and give a sense of what they're like to be around.

- *Tell the reader what the character* does *while they talk.* There are lots of examples of this technique in *Quest for the Crystal Crown.* Instead of just writing *said* next to every piece of dialogue, write what the character *does.* This helps bring the scene to life in more detail for the reader and also gives you an easy way to show how the character is feeling while they talk. Here are a few examples of what we mean:

Torian clapped his hands. "Who's ready for some gray pears?!"

Erika nodded. "Eleven years looking for this*?" She spat onto the ground.*

His eyes crinkled in concern. "Maybe not. But we have to try."

- *Tell the reader exactly* how *the character says it.* Here's another way to avoid writing the word *said* over and over again: You can choose words that get more specific about *how* the character says whatever they're saying, so the reader has an easier time hearing it in their head. In this book, for example, there has been dialogue where characters "wailed" and "squeaked" and "snarled" and "huffed"—and that's just the beginning! Here are a few more examples of words you could use instead of *said*, which you can choose based on *how* the character is talking (we chose these words especially for heroes, who often are in an emergency, or like to brag about their accomplishments, or get annoyed at setbacks, or have to speak quietly so that villains can't hear them):

For bragging about something	For an annoyed character
boasted	argued
bragged	complained
claimed	muttered
exaggerated	whined

For an emergency situation	For speaking quietly
commanded	confided
cried	murmured
ordered	whispered
pleaded	
roared	
screamed	
warned	
yelled	

Here, as always, you have PERMISSION TO GET WEIRD and come up with a totally different way to describe how the character is talking. For instance, in a few chapters, you're going to meet a very disgusting character who says something "in a voice like curdled milk." What does that mean, exactly? It's hard to say, but it sure sounds disgusting! If you have a character who talks in a disgusting voice, compare it to something disgusting. If your character has a beautiful voice, compare it to something beautiful ("a voice like soft rain sprinkling through a sunbeam"). If your character has a loud voice, compare it to something loud ("a voice like a refrigerator crashing into a jet engine"). You get the idea!

IDEA STORM: CREATE A QUEST

Decide on a quest for your own story! What, or who, does the hero need to find to help them solve the Hero-Sized Problem? If you want, feel free to draw a picture of the **quest object** to help spark your imagination. You definitely have PERMISSION TO GET WEIRD.

Be sure to write about how the hero finds out about the quest: Do they read about it in a special book? Does a helper tell them about an old legend? Does the villain taunt them? ("You'll never find where I've hidden the amulet!")

How does the hero feel about going on a quest? Are they terrified? Do they need a helper to motivate them to go? Are they excited? Do they go off with the whole town cheering them on? Or are they nervous someone will try to stop them, so they attempt to sneak out of town before anyone knows they're gone? This is also a great time to include some interesting dialogue. Whether the hero is terrified and giving a panicky rant about what could go wrong, or excited and making a heroic speech, or nervous and whispering their plan to a helper, it will be fun for you to imagine what everyone is saying as the quest begins.

Once your hero has started off, it's time for the **middle** of the story! Keep going!

THE MIDDLE: THE QUEST

CREATE A WORLD: BEYOND THE WALL

As Laura and Millie find themselves outside the walls of Hillview, unable to return, their quest has finally begun . . . which means we are officially in the **middle** of the story. The hero has started their journey into a new, unknown world, where they'll be facing new dangers they've never had to deal with before (like whatever that animal was that started attacking Laura and Millie at the end of Chapter 8—keep reading to find out more about that thing).

As a writer, this is where the real fun begins. While your hero is on their quest, you're going to be planning out lots of **obstacles** to put in their way. An **obstacle** is a smaller problem that comes up while they're on the quest to solve the Hero-Sized Problem, and it could really be anything: a mountain they need to cross, a monster they need to confront, a maze they need to get out of, or even something much, much weirder (we'll give you more examples as you keep reading).

Since the hero is going to be journeying to new places they've never visited before, this is a good time to start thinking again about a **map**!

If you haven't drawn a map yet, you can go back to

"Create a World: Starting with a Map" on page 184 for advice on how to do that. And if you've drawn only a map of the area where the hero starts out, try drawing a bigger map of your world that shows all the places your hero will pass through on their quest. Take a look at the map at the very beginning of the book for an example. The illustrator, Joe Todd-Stanton, used Angie's ideas to create a map of the whole world of Lysoria.

Once you have a map, you can start using it to get ideas about what kinds of obstacles you want your heroes to face. There are three ways you might do this:

- *Look at what you've already drawn.* Do you have a tall mountain, a pool of lava, or a terrifying monster's lair on your map? Pick a dangerous place you want your hero to visit, and come up with more details about what it's like there.
- *Look at the blank spaces.* One of the best places for your imagination to go wild is in the blank spaces on a map. Find a place where you haven't drawn anything yet, and think about what kinds of obstacles your character might find there.
- *Think about the story so far.* Maybe your hero already knows about some of the dangers they'll face. For example, if you know there are Hexors roaming around the land, you can decide where the hero might run into them while on the quest.

Do you want more advice on creating interesting obstacles? Keep reading! There's more on that coming up soon.

CREATE A WORLD: MAGIC

Wizards shooting colored rays out of magic wands! Witches turning heroes into toads! Sorcerers floating in the air and forming interdimensional portals with their hands!

Magic can be a fun thing to write about in a fantasy adventure, but as a writer, you need to decide exactly **how magic works in *your* world.** Hopefully your world is a place that will seem very real to the reader, even though there are very imaginary things, like magic, taking place there. The more you decide *exactly* how that magic is going to work, and figure out lots of details to make it special and interesting, the more real it will seem—and the less it will seem like a copy of the magic in every other story.

As always, in your world the rules are up to you—and if you *don't* want to have magic in your world, that's fine, too: Just skip this part! But if you are planning on including some magic, it can help to ask yourself these questions:

Who can do magic in your world? Is everybody magical,

or are some people magical and some aren't? How do people find out that they're magical? When they're little babies, do they just start burping magical dust one day, or do they need to be trained and learn how to use their magic skills?

How powerful is the magic in your world? In some fantasy worlds, magic is everywhere, with wizards constantly casting powerful spells and evildoers attempting to use magic to control everyone and everything. But in other fantasy worlds, magic is much less common: Very few characters can use it at all, and many characters don't even believe in it. When magic does appear, it's an extremely rare surprise. And then there are worlds like the one in *Quest for the Crystal Crown,* where in the old days, magic used to be very powerful, and the Lysors wielded it to keep the world healthy and beautiful . . . but by the time of our story, magic is much less common, and regular people don't really trust the "small mages" that can use it. Why would a writer choose this kind of world? Well, if magic used to be very powerful, that means it's possible it will be powerful again someday. In fact, maybe by the time the quest is complete, your hero will find out how to use some of that old, powerful magic and really surprise the villain. . . .

What kinds of magic exist in your world? In the world of *Quest for the Crystal Crown,* magic comes from the elements: Certain people have control over fire, or water, or earth, or air. This is a fun kind of magic to write about, but it's far from the only kind of magic possible in a fantasy story. Here are a few other examples:

- *Magic words.* Some magic is all about saying the right words. If you can learn those words, magical power will flow through you, and you'll be able to make all sorts of bizarre things happen: People will transform into animals, furniture will fly through the air, castles will build themselves out of nowhere—whatever you can imagine. These magic words might be in a made-up language ("Blabbity bop, rargy gargy!"), they might be a short poem ("Triple my hair, look at a bear, make the furniture fly through the air!"), and in some stories writers just use words from other *real* languages to be their magic words. (Lots of wizards do their spells in Latin, the language they spoke in ancient Rome. That's not a joke—do a little research on Latin and you might see some words you'll recognize from your favorite fantasy story!)
- *Illusion.* In some stories magic is mostly illusion. A powerful magician can make it seem like the sky is turning green, or that a house has suddenly appeared in an empty field, or that they've turned themselves invisible . . . but as soon as the spell wears off, everything goes back to normal.
- *Telepathy and telekinesis.* Telepathy basically means

having "mind powers." This kind of magic lets people read each other's thoughts, or talk using only their minds, or even try to control another person's mind. Another kind of mind power, called "telekinesis," means being able to lift, or throw, or play with objects using only your mind.

- *Healing.* Like Laura's dad, some magic users focus on healing people who are sick, or injured, or who have had an evil spell cast on them.
- *Potions.* Some magic is more like cooking. First you need to find the right ingredient. That might include rare plants, parts of animals, minerals, or even much weirder ingredients ("a single drop of water that has been touched by the sunlight on planet Bailsoap"). Then, you have to cook the ingredients in *exactly* the right way: the right heat, for the right amount of time, with the exact correct number of stirs. . . . Maybe it even matters what day of the year it is, or what room you're in, or what magic words you say as you cook it—there are a lot of weird conditions you can add for how to cook *your* magic potion. And that's not even including what you want the potion to *do:* Transform one thing into another? Cause a snowstorm? Make a song play out of thin air? It's up to your imagination!
- *Portals between worlds.* Some magic is all about

communicating with other worlds—either between a fantasy world and our real world or between different fantasy worlds or different dimensions or distant planets. There are usually ways of traveling between these worlds, as well, and bringing objects, creatures, or even people back and forth between them through some kind of portal. A "portal" can be lots of different things. Sometimes it's obvious, like a glowing circle of light or a machine made to open up tunnels in space. But sometimes it's much less obvious. A portal can be disguised to look like an ordinary door or even to be completely invisible—you don't know it's there until you've accidentally passed right through what looked like a solid wall.

Of course, all those ideas are just scratching the surface—in your fantasy world, magic is all up to you, and you can come up with much weirder kinds of magic than anything listed here.

What's it like when someone is doing magic in your world? When someone is doing magic, what *exactly* does it look like? Does the magic user move their hands or body? Is there light? Or darkness? Does the air shimmer like water, or is there some other unexpected effect? What *sound* does it make? Are there magic words? Does the magic itself make a sound? A fizz? A pop? A high-pitched squeal? A low-pitched rumble? Is there a *smell*? Does it smell like smoke? Chemicals? Rotten tomato sauce? Or can you *feel* the effects of the magic if you're nearby? Is there a gust of wind? Static electricity in the air? The answers are up to you, but the more details you can include about how you experience magic with all five senses, the more real it will all seem to the reader.

CREATE A WORLD: CREATE A CREATURE

Rotslobbers! Draguins! Cyclopopotomuses!

Some of the most fun you can have in writing about a fantasy world is imagining some of the weird, terrifying, hilarious creatures who live there. This is actually really easy to do—since the rules of your world are up to you, you're free to just let your imagination go wild and create the coolest creature you can think of! Does it have huge claws? Big colorful feathers? Can it dig underground? Turn invisible? Is it part robot? Or do you want to just combine two different things together into one creature? Half dragon plus half penguin equals Draguin! Boom—done!

If you're looking for more ideas to get you started, here are a few ways you can get your imagination going:

- *Start with a real animal.* Lots of the creatures we've just met in *Quest for the Crystal Crown* are real creatures combined with imaginary creatures. (For example, there's an imaginary monster from Greek mythology with only one eye, called a "Cyclops." Cross it with a hippopotamus: It's a "Cyclopopotomus"!) In lots of fantasy stories, writers will take a real creature and change it *just a little* to fit in with their fantasy world. Maybe it's a world full of lizards, big and small, so instead of "dogs," they have big friendly lizards that look and act just like dogs called "dizards." Or maybe there's a snake . . . but with legs. Or a whale . . . but it can fly. Or a cat . . . but it's purple. Just start with a real animal, and let your imagination do the rest.
- *Research prehistoric animals.* Millions of years ago, there were real animals walking around on Earth that would look absolutely *unbelievable* to us today. For example, tens of thousands of years ago, there was an animal called the "Siberian unicorn." It wasn't anything like the unicorns we imagine today, with elegant horse bodies and magical horns, shooting out rainbows. No, the Siberian

unicorn was actually a lot more like Donkeycorn. It looked like this:

It was probably very smelly and just as terrible to ride around on as Donkeycorn. Doing a little bit of research, and looking at all the weird prehistoric animals that *really* used to walk the earth, can be a great way to get ideas for creatures in your fantasy setting.

- *The right creature for your world.* Is your world covered in snow and ice? What kind of creature would survive well in the cold? What would their feet and legs need to be like to carry them through the freezing, slippery terrain? Or maybe your world is a gas giant planet, with no solid ground to even stand on. (You have PERMISSION TO GET WEIRD—why not?) What kind of creature could float, or fly, or find a way to live in a cloudy, windy place with no ground? Or maybe you have an idea for a specific part of your world, like the Putrid Forest. What kind of creature would live in a putrid forest? Probably something poisonous and disgusting, like a rotslobber! Think about what your world is like, and figure out what kind of creature would fit in there, whether it's cold, hot, wet, dry, bright, dark, bouncy, sticky, or whatever!

QUEST LOG: HELP FROM AN UNEXPECTED PLACE

A tall man with long limbs and elbows like knotted wood grabbed Quin and dragged him deeper into the barn, the sack still over his head. The man's face was so worn it looked like old leather.

"Trespasser!" he shouted in a raspy voice. He picked up Quin by the belt loops and tossed him into a trough full of filthy water.

On a long, dangerous quest, a hero may need to take help wherever it can be found—even from extremely unexpected places. For example, at first it may have seemed like a big mistake to go asking for help from Hobbly Knobbly. In fact, for a minute it looked like the quest might end right there, with an angry Hobbly Knobbly doing away with the hero and her friends! But then things took an unexpected turn, when he suddenly offered to help them instead.

Hobbly Knobbly is an example of a "Mighty Helper" character. Usually the hero meets this character at an important moment in the story, when they are in desperate need of help or else stuck on how to continue their quest. Just in time, a Mighty Helper appears—but getting help from them isn't always easy. Let's look at how to put a Mighty Helper in your story:

Step 1. *Make up a Mighty Helper for your hero to meet.* There are two ways to go with this. On the one hand, they could be a character who is obviously "mighty" right from the start, like a powerful knight, or a magical being, or a gigantic spirit, or a ferocious talking animal, etc. On the other hand, they could be something weirder and more unexpected. Maybe they don't look so powerful right away, or maybe at first sight they look creepy, or scary—like Hobbly Knobbly, who at first appears to be just an extremely mean and grumpy old man.

Step 2. *Show the reader the character's Mighty power.* Write about the Mighty Helper doing something that shows how powerful they are. It can make your story extra exciting if they seem scary at first. Show the knight cutting solid rock in half with a sword, or show the magical being performing a powerful spell—or even (like Hobbly Knobbly) make the reader think this character is going to hurt the hero.

Step 3. Decide why *they're going to help.* With Hobbly Knobbly, it was pretty easy to get his help, as soon as he saw that Laura and Millie were Lysors. But it's not always so easy! Sometimes it takes much more work to get the Mighty Helper to actually . . . help. Here are a few ways it might go:

- *A test.* Sometimes the hero will have to prove their worth to the Mighty Helper. Maybe they need to solve a problem or go on a mini-quest to show they have what it takes to be a hero. For example: "If you are truly a hero, then go retrieve my enchanted fishing net from the bottom of the sea."
- *An argument.* Sometimes the Mighty Helper doesn't want to help anyone. They're suspicious or just want to be left alone. The hero might need to give a heroic speech, or argue their heart out, or even just stick around for days bothering the Mighty Helper until they finally agree to help, as long as the hero will leave them alone after that.
- *A battle.* Sometimes the Mighty Helper really is up to no good, and unlike Hobbly Knobbly, the hero has to defeat them in some way before they'll

help. It doesn't always have to be a fight: Sometimes the hero might trick them, or trap them, or undo the magic spell the Mighty Helper is trying to use to hurt the hero. In the end, the Mighty Helper realizes that they don't have any choice but to help.

Step 4. *Decide how they're going to help.* Once they finally agree to help, there are lots of ways it can happen. Here are some popular choices:

- *Equipment.* Sometimes the hero receives new, powerful equipment to help them face the journey ahead. This can include magical items, or armor, or potions, or even a new kind of transportation, like Donkeycorn.
- *Healing.* By the time the hero makes it to the middle of their journey, what they (or their friends) need most might be medical attention or time to rest and heal.
- *Training.* There might be new, advanced training for the hero to receive. Whatever the hero's main talent is, perhaps this powerful character is also an expert in that talent and can help the hero acquire new skills.
- *Information.* Sometimes information is the most powerful weapon on a quest. Maybe the hero has gotten stuck and needs new directions about

where to go next. Or maybe there's an important piece of information they will need before being able to complete their quest ("before you walk by the dragon chasm, prepare the dragon's favorite food . . ." or "the Door of Ages will not open, unless you use the following tools . . .").

- *A companion (for a while).* The Mighty Helper may even offer to escort the hero on their quest for a little while. If so, this will be a big help, but it probably won't last forever: It will be more exciting if the Mighty Helper has to stay behind at some point and the hero has to face some of the final dangers of their quest alone.

IDEA STORM: STARTING THE QUEST AND MEETING A MIGHTY HELPER

Send your hero out on their quest! You can start by making a map of some of the new, dangerous places they'll need to travel through. Write about what they see and what they *do* in these new places. Maybe they find some weird or scary new creatures (see page 238), or encounter some amazing magic (see page 233).

Before too long, your hero will probably be in trouble, or feeling scared, or unsure how to keep going on their quest.

This is a great time to put a Mighty Helper in your story! Just like the other important characters, you can start by drawing a picture to brainstorm details about them. Then have the Mighty Helper appear in an exciting way: Maybe they show off their incredible power by helping the hero out of a tight spot, or maybe they do the opposite at first, and try to hurt the hero.

Then, think through the steps we listed in the Mighty Helper section on page 241, and decide how the hero finally gets the help they need. Does the hero find a way to prove themselves worthy or overcome some kind of obstacle? Maybe they even need to defeat the Mighty Helper in some way. Finally, you can think about what kind of help the hero receives, and where they head next on their journey!

QUEST LOG: THE "DO'S AND DON'TS" OF MONSTER FIGHTS (OBSTACLES, PART 1)

Well, folks, we've just arrived at the moment some of you fantasy adventure fans have been waiting for: our first big monster fight. A quest is full of difficult **obstacles** to overcome, and a monster might be the most exciting obstacle of all. Let's review how it went down:

> *The troll grunted and turned, locking his bloodshot eyes on them. He pounded his fist on the bridge and let out an angry shout, revealing a single glistening tooth jutting from his pink gums.*

There was only one thing to do.

> *They all charged the troll with weapons drawn! Quin shot a fireball, and it hit the troll right in the face! Millie kicked the troll. The troll kicked her back. They kept kicking and kicking. Then Laura jumped in the air and head-butted the troll. The troll roared. They kept fighting. Then they fought some more!*

Wait a minute . . . that's not actually what happened in the story! It's definitely what *could* have happened in a monster fight, but things worked out a bit differently here. Why didn't Laura and her friends attack the troll, combining their powers and doing cool special moves to defeat it in combat?

The best way to answer that question might be to take a look at our "do's and don'ts" of writing a good monster fight:

DO write what makes sense for **your characters.** Laura,

Millie, and Quin are kids. Hot Breath is a twelve-foot-tall monster (even though he turns out to be a baby monster). These kids are simply not the kinds of heroes who would take out weapons and charge straight at a troll—and if they did, they'd probably lose (things didn't turn out so well when Quin brought out his fireball, after all). Maybe the heroes in *your* story would love to fight a monster—that's fine! But if your heroes have a weird talent (see the Hero's Talent Challenge on page 202) or if they're simply the kinds of heroes that use their minds to come up with unusual, creative ways of overcoming obstacles, it's definitely okay to have a WEIRD idea for how they get past the monster (like singing it a lullaby). In fact, if your heroes approach the monster in a WEIRD way, it will be *easier* to keep many readers interested! Anytime there's a fearsome monster, everyone expects there to be a big fight—but if you surprise the reader with something WEIRD, you'll really make them sit up and pay attention.

DON'T just list a bunch of fighting moves your characters do. That doesn't mean you can't have the characters fight—it just means you need to make it *interesting* for the readers. On TV or in a video game, it looks cool when a hero does a triple backflip, shoots a laser out of their foot, then unleashes their ultimate power move on a monster. It's not as exciting to read about when it's just a list of those fighting moves. What should you do instead? Well . . .

DO write about what your characters are feeling, and what

they say. If the characters are fighting a big, scary monster, they're probably going to feel scared! Or maybe angry or surprised—or even excited. If your reader can feel those emotions along with the characters, they are going to be much more interested in the fight. So even if your hero does a triple backflip, shoots a laser out of their foot, and then unleashes their ultimate power move on the monster . . . in between those things, let the reader know how the hero is *feeling.* You could describe how the hero's muscles ache as they attempt a difficult move. Or if the monster is fighting back, write down exactly what the hero sounds like as they cry out in surprise and try to dodge the attack ("UNNNNNNGGGGG!"). Another great way to show how the hero is feeling is with **dialogue** ("I sure hope this works!" or "Arrgg! I think we're done for!" or "Watch this, it's triple flip time!"). For more on this, you can review the "Create a World: Dialogue" entry on page 225!

DON'T be afraid to make things go wrong for your hero. This is the most important tip we can give about monster fights—or about *any* kind of obstacle your characters might face. If things keep **going wrong** for the heroes, it will be much more interesting to read about than if they keep landing awesome moves against the monster over and over without breaking a sweat. For example, check out the "Make It All Go Wrong" sheet on page 251 to see how it went when Laura and her friends met the troll.

Lots of things can go wrong in a monster fight. Maybe

the bridge catches on fire . . . or the monster eats the hero's sword . . . or the kickboxing hero trips and falls on her back . . . or something much weirder that you haven't thought up yet! This is true no matter what the obstacle is: Maybe the heroes are trying to climb a mountain in a storm, or cross a fast-moving river at night, or find their way through a maze deep underneath a castle. It will be much more interesting to see them deal with the obstacle if something **goes wrong** with their plan and they have to scramble to figure out a new plan.

MAKE IT ALL GO WRONG

What is the obstacle?

Laura and her friends need to get across a bridge—but a troll is guarding it!

What is the first thing your character tries to get past the obstacle?

Laura, Millie, Quin, and Donkeycorn try to run away.

What goes wrong? How do things get worse?

The troll is too fast for them! He gets in front of them, and now he's mad. He's shaking the bridge to try to throw them off! Donkeycorn is puking!

What is the next thing your character tries to get past the obstacle?

Quin tries to fight the troll with fire magic.

What goes wrong? How do things get worse?

The bridge catches on fire!

What is the next thing your character tries to get past the obstacle?

Millie realizes that the troll is actually just a giant baby troll. He needs a nap—so Millie sings him a lullaby.

Does it go wrong? Or does your character get past the obstacle?

It works! The troll falls asleep, and they get across the bridge!

QUEST LOG: GETTING WEIRD (OBSTACLES, PART 2)

Not all obstacles involve fighting monsters, or climbing huge mountains, or swimming through shark-infested waters. Some obstacles are just . . . weird. For example: In order to get Deirdre to use her magic powers, Laura and her friends needed to *make her cry*.

A great way to shake things up and have your story take an unexpected turn is to come up with a weird obstacle. Will your characters need to melt a giant block of ice? Figure out how to speak with a bird? Enter a labyrinth filled with three thousand plastic pumpkins and not be allowed to leave until they locate the one genuine pumpkin hidden in the middle? There isn't a wrong answer; this is all about letting your imagination get as WEIRD as possible.

Once you have a weird obstacle, it's tons of fun to decide what weird solutions your characters will come up with to get past it. For example, to make Deirdre cry, Laura and her friends told a terrible joke, attempted to tickle her, and then finally made it happen by using a slightly eaten onion. How often can you get past an obstacle with a slightly eaten onion? It takes a *weird* obstacle to set up a solution that weird!

QUEST LOG: BAD CHOICES (OBSTACLES, PART 3)

Sometimes the most exciting kinds of choices are *bad* ones. For example, you've probably read the sort of story where the main character is walking down the street, sees a dark scary house with a dark scary door, and then for some reason decides to go *inside.* You're screaming at the character, "No! Don't do it! Don't go in there!"

It's exciting to read about—but also kind of annoying, because you can't help wondering, "Why would you go in there? What is *wrong* with you?" It doesn't always make sense when a character makes a really bad choice like that. There is an easy way to get around this, however, and get all the excitement of a character doing something really dangerous, and none of the annoyance of wondering *why* they're doing it: Just give the character nothing but **bad choices.**

Sometimes in an adventure story, the hero will have to decide which way to go in their journey, and no matter what they choose, there will be a life-threatening obstacle in their way. Will you take the road through Bog Belly or the Putrid Forest? Will you take the path over the freezing, stormy, dangerous mountain or through the deep, dark, monster-infested cave? Will you sail your boat past the monster that will grab and eat your crew or the monster that will suck your whole boat underwater?

This is exciting for the reader, and it also makes sense why the hero is choosing to do something dangerous: They have no good options! If they want to complete the quest, they need to decide which choice seems the least terrible and hope for the best.

IDEA STORM: OBSTACLES

It's time to put some obstacles in your hero's path! Check out our three obstacle entries on page 246, page 252, and page 253 to get some ideas!

There are also more places you can flip back to, to help you brainstorm! Do you want to create an interesting monster for your heroes to face? Try going back to the "Create a Creature" entry on page 238. You can follow the advice in that section to help you create a weird, detailed monster that nobody has ever heard of before.

Or maybe you want to give the hero some **bad choices** and send them to a really nasty, scary place like Bog Belly. This would be a great time to review some of the "Words for Places That Are . . ." way back on page 191, to help you perfectly describe the stinky, or scary, or foggy, or just plain weird place that you're planning to send the hero.

Or let's say you have an idea for a really WEIRD obstacle, but you wish you'd done it earlier in the story. Can you go back and add an obstacle before the hero ever meets the Mighty Helper . . . or even way back in the beginning of the story, before the Hero-Sized Problem appears? OF

COURSE you can! Remember that your story isn't going to start out perfect: Add a new page, or cross something out, or squeeze in a new obstacle anywhere you want! The rules are all up to you.

Finally, if your heroes are arriving at a really scary, weird location where there are going to be lots of obstacles, it will help bring that place to life if you use as many **details** as possible. Keep reading for ideas about how to do that. . . .

CREATE A WORLD: IT'S ALL IN THE DETAILS

Bloato's Goblin cave is a disgusting and terrifying place, and what really brings it to life are the **details.** Whether you are writing about a scary goblin cave or somewhere completely different, thinking about *lots* of details will help to make it seem like a real, unique, interesting place for your reader.

Here are a few questions you can ask yourself to help you brainstorm **details** about a place in your own world:

- *Where do people live?* Depending on your setting, people might live in cottages, or castles, or giant space stations orbiting distant stars. In the case of these goblins, they live in a setting that suits them well: a big dark cave, on the edge of a disgusting bog.

- *How do people spend their free time?* We learned several fun details about what goblins do in their free time, including playing a game called Ruby Toss (which you can win either by tossing a ruby into a goblet or by accidentally knocking someone out), doing a dance called the Gobtrot, and making goblin wax candles, which they do by . . . well, if you read Chapter 17, we don't need to repeat it here (it's gross). For your world, you could invent sports, or music, or books people read, or products they make, or toys they play with—anything that fits the place *you're* writing about.
- *What do they eat?* The goblins eat a lot of things at "feasting hour," and most of them are surprisingly tasty—everything from "salted cheeses" to fruit, to meat, to "chunky soups." We also learn *how* the goblins eat, which is without any table manners. (*"Forget finger food—this is face food!"*) In your setting, you could choose to have delicious food, disgusting food (like the "Thew" that Millie cooks), weird food, enchanted food (which casts some sort of spell when you eat it), etc. Be sure to describe how the food smells, the texture in your mouth, and any other details that will help to bring it to life for the reader.

- *How do people get around?* We don't learn much about this question for the goblins, but in many stories, it will be important to think about the transportation people use. Do they ride giant sleds over miles of snow? Do they use submarines to get back and forth between underwater caves? Do they have specially designed rockets that launch out of volcanoes? Do they ride weird animals? Again, the only right answer is the answer that fits the world *you're* writing about.
- *Who is in charge?* And what would Bloato's cave be like without Bloato himself? Greedy, selfish, disgusting Bloato, with his jiggling belly and the silk tablecloth that he uses to blow out the green mucus from his nose (ewwwww). Knowing something about who's in charge can tell you a lot about the people who live in the place you're writing about. Are they scared of their leader? Do they love their leader? Is something wrong with their leader? Does their leader rule by strength or by magic, or are they elected or chosen in some way? Your answer will be very different depending on the kind of world you want to create!

THE END: THE RETURN

QUEST LOG: COMPLETING THE QUEST

. . . *down, down, down into the darkness.*

The **end** of a story often starts in darkness.

In your story, the heroes might not be in an actual deep dark cave like Laura and her friends, but usually things are not going so well. They might be captured by monsters . . . or yelling at their friends . . . or suddenly realizing that there's one last GIGANTIC obstacle in their path, and they don't know how to get past it . . . or like in *Quest for the Crystal Crown*, it may be a little bit of all those things. This is called the **darkest hour** in a story: Your characters are at the lowest, most difficult point in their journey, and it's starting to look like they'll *never* complete the quest.

But then, something happens.

A new character might appear to lend your characters a hand when they need it most . . . or they might suddenly realize how they could use some equipment the Mighty Helper gave them . . . or perhaps they figure out a plan to work as a team and combine their talents to move forward, out of their darkest hour.

Once you get that far, writing the end of the quest is actually simple: You decide on a final, GIGANTIC obstacle for the heroes to get past in order to complete the quest.

Besides being GIGANTIC, this obstacle can look a lot like the ones we've already looked at:

Do the heroes get into the biggest monster fight of their lives or deal with another GIGANTIC obstacle where things keep **going wrong**? See Obstacles, Part 1 on page 246 for more details!

Do you want to blow the reader's mind by making this obstacle the **weirdest,** most unexpected thing they've ever seen? See Obstacles, Part 2 on page 252 for more details!

Or maybe you want to turn up the tension by giving the hero nothing but **bad choices:** No matter how they approach the final obstacle, it seems hopeless . . . so they decide on one terrible choice and try to do their best. See Obstacles, Part 3 on page 253 for more details!

And then . . . THEY FINISH THE QUEST! The Crystal Crown (or whatever the quest object is in your story) is theirs!

Is that it? Is everything over? In most stories, the characters aren't quite done yet. Keep reading. . . .

QUEST LOG: MEANWHILE, BACK AT HOME . . .

The heroes have finished the quest! Happily ever after, the end!

Oh wait—in all the excitement we forgot about something very important: The heroes are still far from home, and they have unfinished business to take care of. That could include one or both of these things:

1. *The Hero-Sized Problem still hasn't been solved!* Maybe the hero was on a quest to find an object, or a person, or some knowledge to help them solve the problem . . . but now they have to use what they've gained on the quest to actually *solve* it. You can write about what happens when they finally, finally have their chance to return and save the day!
2. *The hero discovers a new problem at home.* In some stories, the hero completes the quest, only to arrive home and discover a whole new problem that came about while they were gone. Maybe a villain has infiltrated the town . . . or there's a new natural disaster . . . or their family is in danger . . . or something much weirder! The hero will need to use the new skills, or friends, or items they've acquired on their quest to help confront this new danger.

Either way, dealing with one more big problem is a great

way to cap off an adventure story and give the hero, and all their new friends, a moment to shine one more time in an exciting scene. In fact, you're about to read a scene just like that in *Quest for the Crystal Crown*. . . .

CREATE A WORLD: SURPRISES (SPOILER ZONE)

Did you see that one coming?

Who would have thought that all this time, kindly mayor Torian was behind this whole mess?!

By the end of your story, the reader has been in your world for a while, and they've seen a lot of what that world has in store. That's why it's a good idea to keep a couple of **surprises** waiting, to keep them entertained until the very end of the story.

A surprise can be anything—maybe it's something you've decided about the world from the very beginning but have kept *hidden* up until now. Maybe it's something you think up only right at the end of the story, and you add it in to pump up the excitement.

Maybe a character who the hero thought was a friend turns out to be a terrible villain (like Torian). Maybe you create a new, incredible creature or monster, more dangerous than anything the reader has seen so far (like the giant rat). Maybe a new character appears, who offers desperately needed help (like Laura's mom). Maybe an old friend reappears right when the heroes need them most (like Hobbly Knobbly). Maybe a character who has been around for the whole story suddenly reveals a hidden strength or power (like Donkeycorn finding its unicorn magic). Maybe the island the characters have been visiting on their quest was actually a gigantic egg, and a sea serpent a mile long hatches out and goes speeding into the ocean. (That didn't happen in this story . . . but it would sure be surprising!)

All those ideas are just the tip of the iceberg of possibilities, and as with everything else: There's not a right or wrong type of surprise to put into your story. It's all about what would work best for the world that *you're* creating.

QUEST LOG: AN ENDING FIT FOR A HERO

The crown has been returned (and destroyed). The Lysors and Hexors are rebuilding Hillview together. The quest is complete. Where do we go from here?

There are lots of different ways to end a story, but in an adventure story, there's usually a big focus on how things turn out for the hero. Here are a few popular options:

- *Become a leader.* Now that your hero has saved a huge number of people, those people might be so grateful that they decide the hero should be put in charge! Maybe they elect the hero mayor, or crown the hero as queen, or invent a whole new job where they put the hero in charge of keeping the community safe.
- *Retire/relax.* Going on a quest is hard. Some heroes just want to live a quiet life when it's all done—or at least take a long, well-deserved break. Heroes might go on a vacation or go to live for a while in a quiet little place in the woods. Some heroes are even so tired of being a hero that they change their names and go into hiding, so that everyone will stop congratulating them or asking them for help on a new quest.
- *Look for a new adventure.* Once they get a taste for adventure, some heroes just want more! They leave their home once again, looking for more problems that need solving and more quests that need a hero to accomplish them. Or else the hero begins training and honing their skills for the next time trouble rears its head.
- *Paying the heroic price.* To be a hero means to care about something bigger and more important than yourself and to help save people no matter the cost. Some heroes give up their lives to make the

world a better place—and for some writers, this is the most exciting, dramatic, or realistic way to bring the quest to a close: The hero sacrifices themselves to save the world and is remembered in legend forever afterward.

- *Fulfill their biggest dream in life.* Laura became an explorer . . . and not only that, she fulfilled a dream she hadn't even dared to hope for: She found her mom again! Having your hero accomplish a big dream can be a great way to wrap up a hero story—so you may want to refresh your memory about the "biggest dream in life" you came up with way back on the Hero Creator (page 201). As the story wraps up, it can be fun for readers to finally see the hero playing with that cool pet they've been obsessed with . . . or finally tasting the greatest ice cream in the world . . . or finally getting a chance to focus on their basketball career!

IDEA STORM: FROM THE DARKEST HOUR TO THE LIGHT OF VICTORY

Now it's time to finish your story!

How are your characters going to reach their darkest hour? Will they be trapped, or defeated, or lost in a terrifying place? Are they scared, depressed, or so angry they're screaming at each other? Do they feel like they're *never* going to accomplish their goals? Once again, this is a great place to use some **dialogue** (see page 225) to help show the reader exactly how terribly the characters are feeling.

Then . . . how do they turn things around? Does a new character show up to lend them a hand? Do they figure out that it's finally time to use a piece of equipment they've been carrying, or recall a piece of advice given to them at the beginning of their journey? What GIGANTIC obstacle do they get past to finally complete the quest?

Once they complete the quest, does your hero still have a problem to deal with? Maybe they use the quest object to finally solve the Hero-Sized Problem—or maybe they travel back home and find a whole new problem threatening their community. Either way, it's time for a big finish! Decide on some things that go VERY WRONG as they try to solve the problem (check back on page 251 for the "Make It All Go Wrong" chart), and plan some big **surprises** for your reader at the last moment. Will there be a hidden villain? Will an old friend or a Mighty Helper show up again at the last second? Will your heroes meet the strangest, scariest monster they've seen so far? You have PERMISSION TO GET as WEIRD as you want!

When all that's finally finished, decide on an "Ending Fit for a Hero" after a job well done.

This was the last Idea Storm. Did you do them all? If so . . .

Congratulations!

You just wrote a fantasy adventure story!

If you followed along the whole way, then you:

- Wrote about an imaginary world, and the imaginary people who live there
- Put a hero character in that world
- Created a Hero-Sized Problem and maybe a villain with a Villainous Plan
- Sent the hero off on a quest
- When things were getting tough, sent a Mighty Helper in to help the hero
- Created weird obstacles and made sure things went wrong for the hero
- Plunged the hero down into a darkest hour . . . before finally finishing the quest
- Sent the hero back home to get rid of that Hero-Sized Problem
- Finally reached an Ending Fit for a Hero

What can you do now?

Go back to the beginning, and make your story even better! Make your dialogue more exciting, your magic spells more magical, your darkest hour darker, and your obstacles full of even more things going horribly wrong!

OR

Make a totally NEW imaginary world, with weirder creatures, scarier problems, and the prettiest rainbow castles in the universe!

OR

Take a break! Do the Gobtrot! Eat a slice of gray pear pie—you've earned some time off. But if inspiration strikes . . . feel free to draw a new map and see where your imagination takes you.

APPENDIX:

ANGIE'S ORIGINAL IDEA (WITH SPOILERS!)

Here's the complete idea that Angie originally submitted for *Quest for the Crystal Crown*. If you haven't read the whole story yet, ARE YOU SURE YOU WANT TO READ THIS? Because there are spoilers. Don't say we didn't warn you. It's still not too late to turn back!

Okay, here it is (she submitted this along with the map she drew, which you probably already saw on page 184):

EVERY GREAT FANTASY ADVENTURE BEGINS WITH A SPARK!

THE MAIN CHARACTER

What is the name of the main character of this story?

Laura

What are some details we should know about them?

Laura is a twelve-year-old girl who lost her mom, an explorer, when she ventured outside her town so she lives with her dad. Laura is a magical creature called a Lysor along with the rest of her town. They live in a lost town called Hillview surrounded by walls and nobody has ever gone outside of them. Except the mayor and he keeps that information to himself. Laura longs to see what might be on the other side.

What are some special talents or strengths that this character has?

Laura loves adventure. Every day after school she tries to look through the thin cracks in the wall to see what's on the other side.

What is the main character's biggest dream in life?

Laura wanted to be an explorer just like her mom.

THE PROBLEM

There is a huge *PROBLEM* that is threatening lots of people in the *FICTIONAL WORLD!*

What is the problem?

One day while Laura was looking through the cracks, she saw enchanted arrows being shot at the walls so Laura tried to warn the town that something wanted to come in but nobody listened to her, not even her own dad. Everyone thought that if something was wrong, the mayor, who only Laura doesn't trust, would tell them. A few weeks later, something breaks down the doors and threatens the lost town to destroy everything. Laura would do anything to save her home.

Who is causing the problem? Why?

The person who broke down the door was actually a helper of the mayor who secretly was a monster. He planned to rid the town of its people so he and his minions could take control. They think that it was the village that took their valuable crystal crown when it was actually an evil goblin.

THE QUEST OBJECT

The main character has to go on an adventure to find a special object that solves the huge *PROBLEM!*

What is the object? (The object probably is very rare and has something very special about it! Feel free to describe it in detail—and even add a drawing if you like!)

To save her town, Laura has to go outside of the walls and experience new sights and meet new friends to help her along the way. Her goal is to retrieve the crystal crown (which is powerful beyond the strongest mind and could give unlimited power to its user) and save her desperate village from total destruction. In the end, Laura realizes that she reached her dream and also saved her home sweet home.

A MESSAGE FROM ANNABETH AND CONNOR

One of the most fun ways to start writing a story is to come up with the BIG IDEAS first—and then discover the rest along the way! Angie came up with so many amazing BIG IDEAS that she set us up to write a really exciting story. But there were still a lot of questions to answer and new details to invent. For instance, Angie had the BIG IDEA that a goblin stole the Crystal Crown. Then we had to figure out WHO the goblin was and WHY he stole the crown. (We also had to figure out how many turkey legs the goblins could eat during a single feast!) Angie also had the BIG IDEA that monsters were threatening the town of Hillview. Then we got to invent WHO the monsters were and WHY they were threatening the town. There were a lot of different questions that we answered while writing the book. No matter what, we always came back to Angie's BIG IDEAS for inspiration. So even if you have questions about some of your own BIG IDEAS, you can still start writing. You'll be surprised at how much you can learn along the way.

The STORY PIRATES

CEO: Benjamin Salka
Creative Director: Lee Overtree
Story Pirates Leadership: Greg Barnett, Amanda Borson, Glynis Brault, Duke Doyle, Amy Fiore, Graeme Hinde, Quinton Johnson, Will Kellogg, Katie Kerins, Sherry Layne, Peter McNerney, Sam Reiff-Pasarew, Jacob Ready, and Lauren Stripling.

ACKNOWLEDGMENTS

We would like to especially acknowledge our Education Director Quinton Johnson, whose brilliant pedagogies underlie the Fantasy Creation Zone, and without whom the Story Pirates would not be teaching creative writing in such a dynamic, engaging, and effective way.

We would also like to thank the following friends, colleagues, and champions (in no particular order): Stephen Barbara, Eve Attermann, Derek Evans, Charlie Russo, Sam Forman, Adrienne Becker, Laura Heywood, Allen Hubby, Eric Cipra, Jon Glickman, Natalie Tucker, Nicole Brodeur, The Drama Book Shop, Upright Citizens Brigade, WME, Gimlet Media and Spotify, Geoff Rodkey, Jacqueline West, Hatem Aly, Rhea Lyons, Mark Merriman, Marcie Cleary, Mara Canner, Joanna Campbell, Erica Silverman, Bridgett Spier, Martha Carmody, Blake White, Wendy Zweig, Staci Intriligator, Miguel Ortiz, Elmwood Elementary School, Austin Sanders, Brandon York, Andrew Miller, Gabe Pacheco, Amy Gargan, Bailey David Johnson, Bekah Nutt, Lynn Weingarten, and the hundreds of thousands of kids who have sent us their stories since 2004.

MORE REAL KIDS' IDEAS TURNED INTO REAL BOOKS!

Praise for
The STORY PIRATES Present STUCK IN THE STONE AGE

★ "As smart as it is entertaining."
—*Publishers Weekly*, starred review

★ "A must for young writers . . . and a fab, fun writing manual for writing teachers everywhere."
—*Kirkus Reviews*, starred review

"A nonstop, page-turning adventure."
—Adam Gidwitz, *New York Times* bestselling author of *A Tale Dark and Grimm* and Newbery Honor book *The Inquisitor's Tale*

"So zany and imaginative, it's no surprise an actual kid inspired it."
—Tim Federle, author of *Better Nate Than Ever*

The STORY PIRATES present

DIGGING UP DANGER

BASED ON AN ORIGINAL IDEA BY REAL KID
PHOEBE WOLINETZ

NEW YORK TIMES BESTSELLING AUTHOR
JACQUELINE WEST

Illustrated by HATEM ALY

Praise for
The STORY PIRATES *Present*
DIGGING UP DANGER

★ "It's a fantastic, step-by-step guide with prompts, ideas, definitions, and forms for aspiring Edgar winners. West's tale, decorated with Aly's eerie, cartoon art, is well worth reading on its own—the writing manual takes it to a whole other level."
—*Kirkus Reviews*, starred review

"The caper is charged with chills,
thrills, and even funny twists;
the technical advice . . . is spot-on."
—*Booklist*

"What a fantastically fun
way to learn about writing a story!"
—Chris Grabenstein,
#1 *New York Times* bestselling author

DO YOU WANT MORE STORY PIRATES IN YOUR LIFE?

Check out our free podcast! You can hear additional stories written by kids just like you, performed by the hilarious Story Pirates and friends. PLUS: we interview real kid authors about their writing process!

Find out why the *New York Times* and *Today* call it one of the best podcasts for kids.

Download the Story Pirates Podcast today on any podcast app—or ask your parents to say "Story Pirates Podcast" into their smart speaker!